Step-Chain

All over the country children go to stay with step-parents, stepbrothers and stepsisters at the weekends. It's just like an endless chain. A step-chain. *She Wants War?* is the eleventh link in this step-chain.

I'm Joe, and because of my dad, I'm stuck living with a bunch of girls. There used to be just him, me, and the footie. Now I'm angry with Dad and I'm at war with Eleanor. I don't know how it happened really. I mean, I liked Eleanor — until I had to live with her. I'm giving it six months, then I'm out of here.

Collect the links in the step-chain! You never know who you'll meet on the way . . .

Step-Chain

SHE WANTS WANTS WAR?

Ann Bryant

 EGMONT

First published in Great Britain 2003
by Egmont Books Limited
239 Kensington High Street
London W8 6SA

Copyright © 2003 Ann Bryant
Series conceived and created by Ann Bryant
Cover illustration copyright © 2003 Mark Oliver

The moral rights of the author and cover illustrator have
been asserted

Series editor: Anne Finnis

ISBN 1 4052 0595 4

1 3 5 7 9 10 8 6 4 2

Typeset by Avon DataSet Ltd, Bidford on Avon, B50 4JH
(www.avondataset.co.uk)
Printed and bound in Great Britain by
Cox & Wyman Ltd, Reading, Berkshire

CONTENTS

Step-Chain

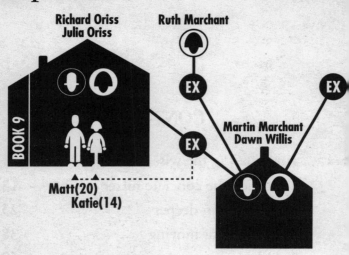

BOOK 9

Richard Oriss
Julia Oriss

Ruth Marchant

Martin Marchant
Dawn Willis

EX

EX

EX

Matt(20)
Katie(14)

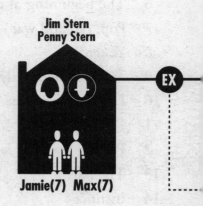

Jim Stern
Penny Stern

EX

Jamie(7) Max(7)

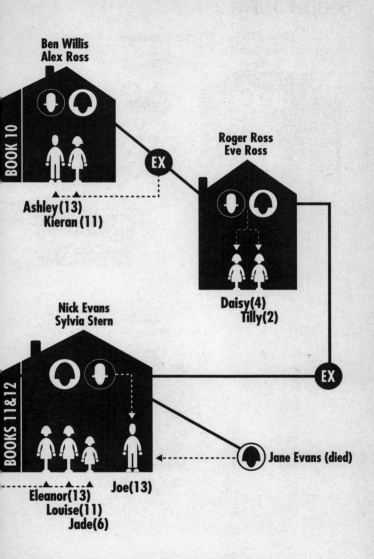

Ben Willis
Alex Ross

BOOK 10

Ashley(13)
Kieran (11)

Roger Ross
Eve Ross

EX

Daisy(4)
Tilly(2)

Nick Evans
Sylvia Stern

BOOKS 11&12

EX

Eleanor(13)
Louise(11)
Jade(6)

Joe(13)

Jane Evans (died)

Read on to discover all the links . . .

1 SUFFERING THE WISE CRACKS

'So what d'you watch last night?'

That's Jack, and he's looking at me. I'm feeling quite smug because Dad and I have got satellite TV. It's just about the only luxury we *have* got, but still . . . 'The match on Sky,' I tell him, grinning.

'Yeah, OK, you don't have to rub it in,' says Andy.

Dean's writing away like a maniac, trying to get his French homework done before the bell goes. He always leaves everything till the last minute, Dean does. He still manages to talk though. 'Did you see *The Grotes*?'

Oh great! I'd forgotten that stupid programme was on last night.

'Wicked, wasn't it?' says Andy, leaning forward. 'What about that bit when Mac left those sweets lying around where he knew his sister would nick a few?'

Dean stops writing and looks up. 'Yeah, the look on her face when she tastes them!'

'Imagine being Mac Grote, and having to put up with a twin sister. It'd be gross, wouldn't it?' says Jack, pulling a face, then giving me an over-the-top grin from point blank range.

Now I'm in for a load of mickey-taking. I wouldn't care if it was about something else – anything but *this*.

I try and get them back. 'Ha ha! Very funny. Don't you get fed up with cracking the same jokes all the time?' I know I'm on to a loser.

Dean's got this clever look on his face. 'Just think,' he says, 'once your dad's moved in with

Eleanor's mum, us lot won't *have* to watch *The Grotes* on Sunday nights. We'll just come round to your place and watch you and Eleanor.'

The others fall about. I ought to ignore them and wait till they get bored with the subject, but it's not easy when you're mad.

Ever since Dad broke the news to me that he and his girlfriend were planning on moving in together, I've had to put up with these wise cracks. I wish I'd never told my mates. I don't know how much longer I can put up with it. It's bad enough having to move in with a bunch of girls, especially when one of them's the same age as you, but it makes it ten times worse when your mates think it's one big laugh. It's not that I don't like Eleanor Stern – I do. And if she'd always been my stepsister I'd be fine with it. But she hasn't. So now it seems like a big deal – this 'moving in together' thing. I tell you it makes you feel a right ponce.

'You're only jealous!' I say.

'Oh yeah, like I'd rather live with Eleanor Stern and her fat-cheeked sister than live with two brothers!' That's Jack.

'Well, I'd swap Eleanor Stern with my sister any day,' says Andy.

We all crack up because it's no secret that Andy fancies Eleanor like mad, and his big sister drives him nutty.

He goes red and turns on Dean. 'I don't know what *you're* laughing at! You've got a sister the same age as Eleanor *Stern's* sister!'

So then Dean looks a bit embarrassed too, and I'm feeling quite pleased with the way I'm getting off the hook here. Until . . .

'Wooo! Look who it is!' Jack again.

My heart sinks. Kelly Grey, from the same class as Eleanor, is standing in our classroom doorway, grinning all over her stupid face.

'She so fancies you, Joe!' Andy whispers into the back of my neck.

'Well, I don't fancy *her*!' I snap back,

pretending to look for something in my school bag.

'She's coming over!' says Dean, grinning. 'This is going to be good.'

My whole body groans. Kelly Grey wears tonnes of black stuff on her eyes and it's obvious she dyes her hair because you can see two different colours. She's got a stud in her tongue too.

'Hiya. What are you lot talking about then?'

'Joe and Eleanor moving in together,' says Jack.

'Not us. Our parents,' I snap.

Kelly comes and puts her arm round me. Gross. 'Leave him alone,' she says in this really drippy voice. 'You've upset him now.'

I can feel her left boob pressing against my arm and it's making my face hot. 'Get off, Kelly. I'm OK.'

'You've gone red, Joe,' says Andy.

He can talk.

She moves her arm, thank God, but she's still determined to embarrass me. 'Don't listen to them, Joe. It'll be nice at Eleanor's. And you'll have a brand new mum, won't you?'

I feel like someone's rammed a knife into my stomach. 'I'm going to the toilet.'

Nobody says a word as I go striding off, but when I'm halfway to the door I hear Dean hissing at Kelly, 'What d'you have to say that for?'

Then she starts protesting like mad. 'What? I'm only saying what Eleanor said. What's wrong with that?'

I don't go the toilet – just walk round for a bit, thinking. How dare Eleanor Stern say that! I thought she was quite nice . . . until now. I don't want a new mum. I never will. It's more than two years since my mum died but I still get this stabbing thing sometimes, and that's what's just happened, only worse than usual.

If Eleanor Stern thinks *her* mum's going to take the place of mine, she can bug off. It's bad enough just *thinking* that. But going round telling people – that's gross.

I just wish Kelly stupid Grey had never come into our classroom. She's ruined everything now. Eleanor's mum is Dad's girlfriend. She's OK. I like her. But she's just Sylvia to me, and that's all she'll ever be.

At home later, I'm eating egg and chips with Dad and letting him know he's ruining my life.

'You don't know what it's like, Dad. Dean and the others take the mick the whole time about me and Eleanor living together. Why can't you and Sylvia just keep going out with each other?'

'What? You mean till *you* say it's OK for us to move in?'

He's twisting it to make it sound like I'm the selfish one. Right . . . 'She's got this stupid friend called Kelly Grey . . .'

'Who has?'

'Eleanor. Who d'you think? And she fancies me . . .'

'Who does?'

He can be so thick sometimes. 'Keep up, Dad. Kelly Grey!'

'Lucky *you*!'

'Shut up! She's hideous.'

He grins.

Can *someone* take me seriously, please?

'I know what's going to happen, Dad. The moment we move in, she'll be round at Eleanor's, getting in my face. It's going to be so embarrassing. Why can't that lot just move here? That wouldn't be half so bad. I'd be more – you know – in control, then.'

'Oh come on, Joe, we've been through this hundreds of times. Sylvia's house is bigger than ours and it's nearer to school and everything. What's the point in her uprooting four of them when there are only two of us to move?'

I feel like telling him what Eleanor's been

going round saying. That'd make him think again. But I don't, because I don't want to bring Mum into this. I can't take that stabbing thing again. No thanks.

'Look, why don't you just come round to Sylvia's?'

'Not that again, Dad.'

'But why won't you? Don't you want to see what your new home's going to be like?'

'No.' How can I explain that it'd make me feel stupid – like a little kid? No, like a visitor. No, more like a refugee. Because it's *their* house. 'They'll show off about it . . . and everything.'

'Eleanor's not like that. You said yourself that she's one of the nicest girls in year eight.'

Yeah, until today.

'And Louise wouldn't know *how* to show off, she's so shy.'

'And ugly,' I mumble under my breath. I know it's cruel the moment I've said it, but I'm mad, OK?

Unfortunately he hears. 'Don't get like that, Joe. I'm not having it. None of us can help our looks.'

I stay quiet.

'Think what it must be like for Louise, having two good-looking sisters and being . . . stuck in the middle.'

'See! You admit it! She's ugly.'

So then he changes the conversation. 'And what about Jade? You haven't even met her.'

'I've told you, I don't want to. She sounds completely off her trolley.'

'She *is* off her trolley. But I swear you'll like her. She's so . . . up front.'

The kid is six and she's up front? What's she going to be like when she's thirteen? What a terrible thought. If we move into Sylvia's I'll have to grow up with Eleanor and the others. Right till I leave home I'll be stuck with them. In my face. The whole time.

I'm back where I started.

He changes tack. 'OK, come and see the house one day when they're not there. They go to their dad's once a fortnight.'

It's not as bad as his last idea.

He's sussed that I'm cracking. 'You'll feel differently once you've seen how much better than our place it is.'

It's true, our place is a bit of a dump. We rent it so we haven't bothered to spend money on it to make it nice or anything. After Mum died Dad was too upset to stay in the house where he and Mum had lived for fifteen years, so we moved here. This place was unfurnished so we brought our own stuff.

I'm saved from answering Dad's question by a knock at the door.

'Come in.'

We both know it's Sylvia. Her smell always comes in first. I think it's hair stuff, but it might be . . . a body thing. I hated it at first, but I'm used to it now.

'Hi!' she says. Then she sits next to me and nicks one of my chips.

I forget all about what Dad and I have been talking about, because Sylvia's so kind of normal and easy to get on with. You don't have to act different when she's around.

'Yes, you may!' I grin.

'May I?' she asks, grinning back.

'Get the report done OK?' asks Dad.

That means Dad must have met Sylvia in her lunch break. They often do that.

She nods and nicks another of my chips. 'May I?' she asks with her mouth full.

'No,' I tell her, pretending to be cross.

'Sorry, Joe.' She looks at Dad. 'How was Mrs Clayton?'

Dad rolls his eyes. He works for himself, fitting gas central heating. Sylvia's talking about one of his customers.

'Still not coughing up what she owes.'

'You're too soft, Nick. You ought to tell her

you won't finish this job till she pays you for the last one.'

'Mm,' says Dad.

But we all know he won't. Sylvia's right. He *is* a soft touch.

And now he's changing the subject. So predictable. 'Nice earrings, Sylv.'

'Thanks. They're not mine. I borrowed them from Ellie.'

Something happens inside my head when she says the name Ellie. I'm remembering what Kelly Grey said, and that gets me mad again. I never thought Eleanor would come out with something like that. I thought she'd realise about Mum. That she's the only mum I'll ever have. No way am I ever having a 'brand new' one.

'I was just trying to persuade Joe to come and have a look at the house,' says Dad.

'Yes, you ought to,' says Sylvia. 'Then you can choose which bedroom you'd like.'

'Aren't you the lucky one!' says Dad, cuffing

me over the head and grinning. 'That's nice of the girls to give you the choice of bedroom, isn't it?'

I don't want them being nice. It makes me feel a right baby. 'I don't care which room I have.'

I scrape my chair as I get up and I can see Dad's about to have a go at me, but Sylvia shakes her head at him so he doesn't.

I go out without saying another word and I know they'll be talking about me in a minute. I can just imagine it . . .

Oh dear. Problems, Nick? I thought Joe was OK about moving.

Don't worry, he'll be fine. He's just had to put up with a bit of ribbing from his friends . . .

Huh! Adults! They don't get it!

2 INSIDE THE CONCRETE MIXER

We're in the canteen, me and Dean and Andy and Jack, and it's this sausage thing that they make with tomato sauce and pasta, and it's nice so we're all quiet. The teacher's on the end of our table, next to Dean and Jack. That's another thing that makes you go quiet. Dinner times are really bad if you get a teacher on the table. They always try and make out they're your best friend, and you just want to tell them to shut up. It's worse than that though because the teachers are all over me at the moment. They must know about me and Dad moving in with Sylvia. Great!

It's Mrs Primett today and she's acting like she really loves me.

'Joe,' she beams, 'would you pass the salt, dear?' The others don't look up. I pass it. 'Have you boys had a good morning?'

Jack grunts. Dean and Andy keep eating. Oh God, it's up to me. I'm just about to come out with a boring reply that might shut her up when I catch sight of Louise Stern by the water.

Oh no! What's she doing here? Year sevens aren't normally in first sitting. They must have got an outing or something.

She's with her mate and they're both staring in my direction. This is not good. Usually the kid looks down if there's any chance at all that she might meet my eyes. Don't say she's decided to speak to me. Dean and the others'll want a ringside seat if she does.

I start answering Mrs Primett's question at a hundred miles an hour. 'Maths was OK, English wasn't very good. We don't like Shakespeare all that much. We've got science this afternoon.'

Jack gives me a look that says, *You got a few pages stuck together or what?*

'You don't like Shakespeare? That's a shame. I find him tremendous fun!'

Her eyes look really big and goggly. It's funny how glasses make that happen. But I can't concentrate on replying because Louise is still staring at me. It's like she's in a trance. Her friend's nudging her and giggling.

'I presume your teacher's just giving you a taste of Shakespeare? Preparation for GCSE, hm?'

Dean looks up. Oh God, he's seen Louise and he's trying to get Andy and Jack to look.

'Er . . . yeah, I s'pose.'

Andy's noticed the girls now, and he's elbowing Jack.

'Is there something going on behind me?' smiles Mrs Primett, turning round to have a look.

The giggly friend's realised there's a teacher watching. She gives Louise a massive elbow in the ribs. Louise comes out of her trance. They both go scuttling back to their places.

Dean and the others are exchanging unsubtle glances and I just know they're revving up for another mickey-taking session the moment Mrs Primett goes. I'm going to have to come up with something to get their minds off ugly Louise Stern and her silly friend.

'Let's go to the art room after this, eh?'

Jack's dead keen. 'Yeah, Mr Hodder said he'd be there all through the lunch break.'

So then we get talking about the monster sculptures we're doing in art, and Mrs Primett asks us loads more questions. I forget about Louise.

I'm a bit ahead of the others going out of the hall, because the dinner lady's taken my plate first. Guess who's waiting for me just outside?

I look the other way and walk past.

'Go on,' says the giggly friend. 'Tell him! Go *on*, Louise!'

'Oi, Joe!' That's Andy. 'I think your stepsister wants a word with you.'

That does it. It's like something's snapped inside my head. I swing round. 'She's not my stepsister!'

'Not yet!' says Andy, grinning.

'Louise wants you to have *her* room when you move in,' says the friend. 'It's got hearts on the wallpaper though and she wants to check that's OK with you.'

Dean and Jack are out of the hall now. They've heard that last bit.

'Hearts! Lovely!' says Jack, cracking up.

Then Andy says, 'Hey, Joe, it'll give you sweet dreams all about Eleanor!'

I'm trying to tell myself that they're only having a laugh but my head feels like it's going to explode and before I know it I'm laying into the kid.

'Look, I don't want your bedroom, all right? I'd rather sleep in a prison cell, OK?' I'm really spitting and there are mottled red bits appearing in her white face, but I don't care. 'Now get lost and take your lippy friend with you!'

I take a step back and she looks different — not ugly any more. Just pathetic. My heart starts hammering. I shouldn't have said that. Her eyes have filled up with tears. Oh God, this is all I need. Now her lip's trembling.

The friend grabs her arm in a stress. 'Come on, Louise.'

But the kid doesn't move. It's like she's rooted to the spot. Really crying.

'What's going on?'

I turn round. It's Eleanor. She's seething.

Kelly Grey's just behind her, looking smug. She's enjoying the show. Some people are like that.

'I said, what's going on?'

'Nothing . . .' I start walking. 'Come on, you lot.'

'What's the matter, Louise?' I hear Eleanor say.

The stroppy friend can't wait to fill her in. 'Louise wanted me to tell Joe that he could have her bedroom if he wanted, because she was too shy to tell him herself. And he started being really horrible and saying he'd rather have a prison cell, and stuff like that.'

By this time Dean and the others have caught up with me.

'Joe!' Eleanor screeches. Sounds like she's wild.

I break into a jog. 'Pretend we're in a hurry!'

'You're for it!' Andy informs me.

I turn on him. 'Don't call her my stepsister in future. It winds me right up.'

'I know,' says Dean. 'You really went for her, didn't you?'

Jack starts laughing. 'At least you won't have to put up with hearts all over your walls.'

I don't reply. It's just a big joke to them. But me — I feel like I've spent the lunchtime in a concrete mixer and I've just climbed out, head banging, legs trembling.

'Joe!' It's Eleanor again and this time she really means business.

'I'll see you in the art room,' I say to the others, hoping they'll get the hint.

'No chance. We're not missing this,' whispers Dean.

So they just stand there.

Eleanor looks like she hates my guts. Her face is shaking and her eyes are flashing. 'I want to talk to you, Joe Evans – alone!'

'See you in the art room,' says Andy, the moron. And off they go.

The moment they're out of earshot Eleanor starts. She's totally wild, shaking with anger. 'How dare you make my sister cry! You've no idea how shy she is. It's taken her all her courage to come anywhere near you!' She's got her hands on her hips and it's obvious there's more to come. 'For your information, she was feeling sorry for you last night, and she told me she might offer you her room. She asked me if I thought you'd mind, and I persuaded her to go for it. What an idiot I was. If I'd known how you were going to thank her, I'd have told her not to come anywhere near you. And now she's in a real state. You make me puke, Joe!'

I feel bad. Guilty. But only for a second because I'm remembering what she's been going round saying about me having a brand new mum. I'm about to have a go at her when her eyes go all hard. 'Mum must be mental letting you and your dad move in.'

That does it. I completely lose it. 'So tell her then! You'll be doing me a massive favour. I've told Dad I don't want to live with *you* lot enough times.'

I've shocked her. Good. She's gone all white. 'I . . . might just do that.' Then she turns and stalks off.

I go to the toilet because it's the only private place round here. I'm knackered. It's like I've had another dose of the concrete mixer treatment. I sit on the lid, leaning forward with my head in my hands. What a total cock-up!

3 GETTING IN DEEPER

By the time I get home I've gone from feeling angry to guilty and back to angry again so many times that I think my head's going to burst.

Dad gets in at quarter past five. I happen to be on angry, so he really cops it.

'For God's sake, Dad, it's hell at school. Can't you dump Sylvia? I mean, I know she's quite nice and all that, but I don't want you going out with someone who's got a pathetic little year seven girl at my school. She's acting stupid with her friend, giggling and hanging around me at break times.'

I stop to take a breath and it flashes up on the big screen inside my head that I've just told him a complete lie.

'Hold on a sec,' says Dad. 'I've only just walked through the door. Give us a chance to sit down.'

He's trying to be jokey and nice to calm me down. It doesn't work.

'And now Eleanor hates my guts just because I told Louise I wasn't that keen on pink hearts.'

Dad laughs, then he looks suddenly serious. 'I hope you didn't really say that to Louise. She's very sensitive and shy, you know. After she first met me, it took her weeks to be brave enough to actually speak.'

Uh-oh. Back to guilt. 'Well, I didn't say those exact words.'

'Good,' says Dad. 'Stick the kettle on. Let's talk it over.'

What's he think he is – a counsellor?

'No! I don't want to talk it over.' *Back to*

anger. 'I just want to forget the whole thing. Why can't we stay here, Dad? If I have to move in with those girls, I'll . . .'

'Yes?'

'Well, let's just say you'll regret it.'

'Don't make threats, Joe. You're overreacting by a mile. I know it's going to be a bit tricky at first, but in about a week you'll be completely used to it. You'll see.'

'So I'm supposed to look forward to moving in with a shy, fat-cheeked kid, her nutty sister and her stressy cow of a sister, am I?'

He looks like he's about to go ballistic but then changes his mind.

'That's a bit cruel.'

'Not from where I'm sitting.'

'I meant the fat-cheeked bit.'

'Well, she is!'

'Look, Joe, no one's expecting you to instantly click with them . . .'

'Yeah, well don't hold your breath, because

I'm not planning on *ever* clicking with them.'

Dad's looking really hacked off and I'm glad. He sounds all glum and knackered. 'Now do you realise why I've been on at you to spend some time at Sylvia's place? None of this would be happening if you'd all got used to each other.'

I don't reply.

He sighs a massive sigh. 'Better get ready for judo. I'll run you up there.'

I don't feel like going to judo, but it'll get me out of this house. I know Dad'll be straight on his mobile to Sylvia the moment he's dropped me off, and Eleanor's sure to have gone blabbing to her mum about that nasty Joe Evans, so I'm going to get it in the neck when I get back. Great. That'll really make my day.

After judo, I'm standing outside in the dark waiting for Dad, who's the last one to collect, as usual. Simon the judo instructor keeps talking to me.

'How's school these days?'

The pits. 'OK.'

'Got exams this term?'

Thanks for reminding me. 'Yeah.'

'What's your favourite subject?'

'Art.'

'Yeah? That was mine too when I was your age.'

Dad's car comes round the corner.

He stops and rolls down his window. 'Sorry, Simon – I got stuck on the phone.'

No prizes for guessing who you were talking to.

'That's OK. See you next week, Joe.'

I get in and wait for the sermon to start.

'Good session?'

'Yep.'

'Sorry I was a bit late.'

Dad's apologising? Weird. He can't have been talking to Sylvia, but if he *has*, I want to know.

'So you got stuck on the phone?'

'Yeah, Sylvia and I have been talking . . .'

'About me?'

'Yeah, and the girls. We know it's tough and all that . . .'

I'm waiting. What's he up to? Playing a clever little game of going in gently then building up to a massive explosion?

'All I can say is that it *will* get better.'

So what's new?

'Did you and Sylvia talk about . . . Louise offering me her bedroom and all that?'

'No, she didn't say anything about it so I didn't either.'

Eleanor can't have told her yet. She probably goes out to Girl Guides or some poncy thing, and she'll get back and tell Sylvia the whole story later. I don't care. I'll just say she's exaggerating.

I go to school the next day feeling determined not to take any lip from Eleanor. The second I walk into the classroom, Dean and the others pounce on me.

'Kelly Grey's been looking for you,' grins

Jack. 'She said to tell you she's got something to ask you.'

'Yeah,' says Dean. 'What's that all about? As if we couldn't guess!'

'She so fancies you, Joe,' leers Andy.

Here we go again. 'Leave it alone, can you? Who's done the geography?'

'Me,' says Jack.

'Give us a lend of your book. I went to judo and forgot all about the homework.'

He hands it over good as gold, but I'm not off the hook yet.

'Yeah, and she wants to know if you're still mad at Eleanor Stern,' says Dean.

I don't bother to reply. Eleanor Stern's not exactly my favourite topic. But then I crack because I can't help being curious.

'What's it got to do with Kelly Grey?'

'Maybe she's getting lined up to move in with you if you decide not to move in with Eleanor,' says Jack.

The other two crease up.

I'm hunched over the geography, copying it out, but I can't concentrate. I can feel myself getting madder and madder.

'Shut up about her, will you?'

'Whooo! Joe's mad because Eleanor got cross with him.'

I try to hang on to my cool. 'Correction. I'm mad because she's a cow.'

'That's a bit much. She's really nice, Eleanor,' says Dean.

'*And* fit,' Andy adds, which makes the other two crease up again.

He puts on this big-eyed, gormless expression. 'What's so funny about that?'

'She's out of your league, Andy,' says Dean.

They're really bugging me now. 'Hold on a sec. Aren't you forgetting something? I'm supposed to be your mate. And that girl you all fancy is acting totally out of order with me.'

'She was only looking after her sister, wasn't she?' says Dean.

'Oh, 'scuse me while I throw up!'

'Well, she *was*.'

There's no time for any more of that because the bell goes and we have to line up.

At break I'm last to go out. I'm just stuffing books in my bag, about to go outside, when someone comes up behind me and puts their hands over my eyes.

'Guess who?' says Kelly Grey.

It's not worth answering. I just rip her hands off me and keep on with what I'm doing.

'That's not very friendly,' she says in her gooey voice. Then she turns sort of serious. 'Joe, I've got something to ask you . . .'

I'm walking towards the door. 'You'd better be quick then.'

'You play guitar, don't you?'

That stops me. It wasn't what I was expecting. 'So?'

'So would you like to join our band?'

I turn round. She's got me interested. Loads of people know I play guitar but only Dean's ever actually heard me play because I'm not exactly Jimi Hendrix.

She's looking all excited now. 'It's for the Children in Need concert. It'll be really good. Chris Counter's in it.'

Chris Counter's in year nine. He's one of those people who everyone likes even though he's just about the best in his class at work, sport, music – you name it. So I'm thinking, what's he doing in a band with Kelly Grey?

She's reading my mind. 'The band thing was my idea in the first place. You see, there are loads of people singing solos and playing piano or whatever for the concert, but no one's thought of having a band.'

'So who else is in it?'

'Well, there's me singing and Chris on piano . . .'

'Yeah?'

'And Vicky Barrows. She's in year nine too. She's another singer, like me.'

'Yeah?'

'And then . . .' She's hesitating like mad.

'Yeah?'

'Well, we needed another singer to help with the backing, because I'm probably going to be the lead, and Vicky suggested Eleanor . . .'

She may as well have stamped on my big toe. 'Eleanor? Eleanor Stern? Forget it!'

'She's quite good at singing . . .'

'I don't care. I'm not being in a band with Eleanor.'

Something goes flitting across her face. I can't describe it, but it's like she's pleased. Only I'm thinking, *That can't be right. Why would she ask me to join the band if she's pleased that I don't want to? Doesn't make sense!*

'Oh go on, Joe. You won't have to talk to her.' Kelly's coming right up to me with this really pleading, pouty look. I can see orange on her face. What does she think she looks like?

I take a step back. 'I don't see why you need someone on guitar anyway, if you've got Chris on piano.'

'No, that's just it. It turns out that Chris is mega on drums. You should hear him! So it'd be better if he played drums instead of piano. Only it's impossible to sing with just drums, obviously. Then Vicky said what about getting someone to play guitar.' She gives me this smug look. 'And I thought about you.'

I roll my eyes. 'I bet Eleanor was impressed with that idea.'

'She said she didn't think you'd agree.'

I start to walk off again, faster this time. 'So why'd you bother asking then?'

Kelly's chasing after me. I can hear her footsteps but I don't turn round.

'Because I don't get how she knows you wouldn't be any good when she's never even heard you play.'

I'm practically at the other end of the corridor, but I swing round. 'What did you say?'

She just looks at me and waits. We both know exactly what she said.

'Are you telling me that Eleanor said I'm not good enough?'

She nods and shrugs.

My blood's boiling now. 'Eleanor Stern can get stuffed!'

She doesn't waste a second. 'So you're in?'

I nod.

'Great! I'll tell Chris. Come to the music room next Monday.'

4 TALKING OF MOVING . . .

That night I have another go at letting Dad know what he's putting me through.

'Eleanor Stern's going round rubbishing me to everyone, you know.'

Dad's reading the paper but his eyeballs aren't moving from side to side, which proves he's not actually taking anything in. He's staring at one spot. Good. I've got him interested. I'll get him to change his mind about moving in with Sylvia if it kills me.

'I wish she'd just leave me alone, you know.'

He doesn't reply and I don't push it. Let him

think about it a while longer. Let him start asking himself a few questions. Let him sweat.

Sylvia phones at about ten and Dad immediately says I ought to be getting to bed. Good. That means he wants to talk about 'the situation'. *Bad luck, Sylvia – you're about to hear what a nasty piece of work your daughter is.*

I go upstairs without a word. I'm under the duvet when it hits me that Sylvia might be telling him about me laying into Louise. So I go back down again to earwig. My ear's pressed right up against the door, but Dad's speaking in the quietest voice known to man, plus he's got the telly on, so it's impossible to hear what he's saying.

At breakfast next morning I get a surprise.

'Eleanor and Louise are under strict instructions to leave you alone. All right, mate? So now you don't have anything to worry about.'

Wow! Sounds like a bit of a result. Wonder

what brought that on. I go back over last night's conversation in my head . . . *'I wish she'd just leave me alone.'*

Oh, *I* get it. Nice one. Only then he goes and spoils it. 'It works both ways, remember. So *you* keep out of *their* way too.'

OK, but just let either of them even glance in my direction!

So at break time and dinner time I can't stop looking round for them. I want to catch them out, then go back and tell Dad they're breaking the rules and making my life unbearable and all that kind of stuff.

'Whoa!' says Andy, as we're standing in the queue. 'What's up with Eleanor Stern? I just glance in her direction and she gives me this big evil then looks the other way.'

'She's playing hard to get!' says Dean, grinning.

Andy goes a bit red.

'I'm joking!' laughs Dean.

'I know!' says Andy.

So then Jack's craning his neck to get an eyeful, but I keep staring straight ahead, because I don't want her accusing *me* of breaking the rules.

'You're right, Dean,' says Jack. 'She really *is* playing hard to get. Look, Joe.'

No way.

'Oh, here comes your biggest fan!' Jack goes on with his running commentary.

Please don't let it be Kelly Grey.

I look up. It isn't. It's Tasha Hollonby. She's one of Eleanor's crowd but she's OK.

Or is she? Right now she's got that expression on her face that all girls wear when they think they're cleverer than you.

'Eleanor says can you stop staring because it's putting her off her food.'

'Who's staring?' says Andy.

'I'm not talking to *you*, dur!'

I clench my stomach muscles.

'Who then?' asks Jack, grinning like a moron.

'Joe.'

Right, show's over. I've had a gutful of this. I start ripping into Tasha. 'You can tell her from me that I wouldn't stare at her if she paid me, because I might catch something.'

Off she goes, whizzing back to report the hot gossip.

'Bit twitchy today, Joe!' grins Dean.

I'm about to tell him where to shove his witty comments when Kelly gets up and wiggles off towards the loos. (She's sitting a few places along from Eleanor.)

'There goes Kate Moss,' says Jack. We all snigger.

Kelly turns round and gives me an over-the-top smile.

'Whoo! She so fancies you!' Jack goes on.

'How many more times? Are you lot going for an originality award or something?'

That shuts them up – for now.

* * *

Anyone can see Dad wants to talk to me. Ever since he came home about an hour ago he's been biting his nails and going off into big frowning sessions. He probably wants to know how it went at school today. If he's looking for a miracle turnaround in my attitude, he's going to be disappointed.

'Er, Joe . . .' *Here we go.* 'You know we fixed the moving-in date for the ninth – a week on Saturday . . .'

I'm starting to sweat. This feels like it's going to be bad. Very bad.

'. . . because Sylvia's lot were going to be at their dad's that weekend. And we thought it would – you know – be better for you if they weren't around . . .'

'Yes,' I say through clenched teeth.

'Well, it turns out that their dad can't have them after all that weekend because he's got some old friends coming over unexpectedly.'

'So?' I interrupt coldly.

He starts gabbling, like he's got to get it all out in under ten seconds or the house'll blow up.

'Well, rather than wait another week we've decided to bring it forward and kind of get it over with, so you lot can all start getting used to each other.' I stare at him. My mouth's hanging open and I don't seem to be able to shut it. 'Jade's really excited,' he winds up.

'Well, good for Jade!' I yell out in my most sarcastic tone. 'Never mind that I'm feeling suicidal, will you. As long as Jade's OK, that's fine.'

'Oh come on, Joe. Give us a break. It can't be as bad as all that.'

'Yes it *is*, Dad. Worse, in fact. I won't be able to hack it.'

He's getting rattled. 'Well, you've got to face it some time. Sylvia and I can't go on snatching odd moments with each other. We want to be together much more than that.'

'I don't care if you go out every night of the week and leave me here all on my own. Just don't ask me to live with those manky girls!' I'm shouting but I can't help it.

Dad's got his pleading voice on now. 'But we'd only be putting it off, Joe. Look, I've told you, once you've been living with them for a couple of weeks it'll be just as though you've always been there. You've been building barriers and it's time they came down.'

Huh! Like Dad thought of that *on his own.*

'You'll still have your own bedroom, which ever one you finish up with. I mean, you think *you're* hard done by, but what about the girls? Two of them are going to have to double up to make room for you, and *they're* not complaining.'

'So let them keep their skanky rooms. I'm staying here.'

'You can't.'

That's it. Two words. Then he rubs his

forehead with his index fingers like I've given him a migraine or something.

'What d'you mean?'

'I've already told the letting agency we're going at the weekend. They said the new tenants would be thrilled because they've been crammed into their parents' house just waiting for us to vacate. And the furniture storage place is happy to take our furniture a week earlier.'

Everything goes still. I can hear the clock ticking. I haven't cried since Mum died, but right now I feel pretty close to it. The only thing that's stopping me is all the anger that's raging round my body. Before I know it I've broken into this horrible sarcastic laugh, and I'm yelling at him in my roughest voice. 'You can't *make* me move.'

Now he looks really angry. 'Oh, grow up and stop being so selfish, will you! We're moving in at the weekend, and that's that!'

Then he gets up and goes out into the back garden, and I sit there, shattered.

In the morning I refuse to go to school, but he yanks me out of bed and tells me to get a grip.

'You don't know what it's like for me!' I scream at him.

'If you feel the same after six months, we'll move out,' he announces calmly.

That shuts me up. He's given me a light at the end of the tunnel. So why didn't he say that last night? Oh, I get it. He must have phoned Sylvia after I went to bed. I can just imagine how it went . . .

Joe's throwing a real tantrum on the moving-in front, Sylv . . .

Tell him we're giving it six months. He'll have got over it by then.

Hey! Good thinking!

When I go downstairs Dad's scoffing his cereal. I make a big thing of getting the calendar, bringing it to the table right under his nose and putting a heavy ring round May 2, which is exactly six months away, and writing **THE DAY** next to it.

Dad keeps eating. 'We'll see,' he says in this mysterious voice, like he's been on a course in crystal-ball gazing.

5 MOVING IN

Saturday morning. There's just me and Dad and Sylvia in the house. The girls are at their dad's for the weekend. His name's Jim and he's got two stepkids of his own. I wish a miracle would happen and the whole lot of them would emigrate to Australia.

Dad and I got up mega early to carry on where we left off last night. I didn't think we'd got much stuff in our house compared to Dean's and Jack's, but it still took ages to pack it all up in boxes and bags. Our furniture – like the table and chairs and all the big things – has gone into storage now. Dad says we'll probably finish up selling it. I don't see why we can't keep it and make Sylvia put *her* furniture in storage. When I told Dad that, he said it was pointless. We've not even brought my bed. I've got to have Eleanor's, and Eleanor's having Louise's, and Louise is going to share the bunk beds in Jade's room.

So now we're here and I hate the place. Hate it.

'We thought you'd probably prefer Eleanor's room,' Sylvia tells me when we go upstairs. *Yeah, I know.* 'It's the biggest room . . .' She looks at the rug. 'Oh! I thought she was planning on having that in her new room. Maybe she changed her mind at the last minute.'

I want to know how come it's never been talked about that Louise offered me her room.

'Whose idea was it for me to have this room?' I ask as casually as possible.

'Well, it was kind of a family decision.

Louise and Jade are quite excited about sharing a room.'

How come I don't believe her?

Sylvia opens one of the doors off the landing. 'This is it.'

I'm staring round, ready to pounce on any trace of Eleanor that might be left behind so I can get rid of it quick. I open the wardrobe. It's completely empty. Good job. I open every single drawer of the chest of drawers. Empty. There's still the bed to examine but I'm not about to do it in front of Sylvia and Dad.

'I've put clean bedding on it,' says Sylvia. I don't look up, but I can tell from her voice that she's seen me looking at it. I expect she and Dad have been having a laugh behind my back.

It makes me sick. 'She can have the rug – I don't want it.'

'That's very nice of you, Joe,' says Sylvia. 'Eleanor will be pleased, I know.'

I want to tell her I couldn't give a flying fart

what Eleanor thinks, but I can't. That makes me mad because I've just realised I'm going to have to watch what I say the whole time from now on, because of Sylvia and *them*. It'll be like living in the Big Brother house – on show every second of the day. Dad had better realise how bad this is. 'Did you remember to bring the calendar?' I ask him pointedly.

He nods and exchanges a look with Sylvia. I was right. He did tell her. Terrific!

When Dad and Sylvia have gone downstairs I decide to have a nose round. I haven't seen the other rooms up here.

It's weird looking at the double bed in Sylvia's room and thinking that from now on Dad's going to be sleeping in there. It's pretty gross having a new partner at his age, so I close that door quickly and go for the bathroom next because it's a bit safer. It won't give me horrible feelings.

Wrong, Joe. The bathroom is hideous. Thank

God it's got a toilet in it, so at least there's somewhere to throw up. The bath and basin and toilet are the colour of luminous mustard and the towels are black and white. They dazzle your eyes. There are coloured balls and puffy spongy things and jars and bottles and candles and crystals and God knows what else. It's doing my head in and . . . Oh no! I don't believe this – knickers!

I rush out and stand there gasping, leaning against the wall for support. It's no good. I can't live in a place with knickers hanging around. But then I get to wondering whose knickers they might be and before I know it I'm back in there having another look. They're black with a yellow bit round the edges and it says POW! on them in yellow. They're definitely not for kids. That means they must be Sylvia's . . . or Eleanor's. Sylvia wouldn't wear knickers with POW! written on them, would she? I pick them up between my finger and thumb and hold them at arm's length.

I'm holding Eleanor Stern's knickers! This is weird. Then something hits me out of the blue and I drop them and rush out.

On the landing I lean against the wall again. Just imagine if Dean and the others were here and one of them went to the toilet and found the knickers. I'd never hear the end of it at school . . .

'*So what knickers is she wearing* today *then, Joe?*'

It's none of their business. I don't want them knowing stuff like that about Eleanor. She's practically my . . .

I slide down the wall and drop my head into my hands. This whole thing's a massive jumble inside my head. I can't sort it out. All I know is that I'm going to have to find reasons why Dean and the others can't come over for the next six months.

When I've recovered I look up and realise the door to the bedroom on the opposite side of the landing is open by about twenty centimetres and I can see a little dog in there. It's just staring straight ahead, but it's definitely real – the eye that I'm looking at isn't a bead or anything. I'm thinking I'd better go easy here. It might be one of these dogs that looks completely docile but when you get near it, it bares its teeth and takes a bite out of your ankle. I once saw a dog like that on telly. So I'm tiptoeing up to the door, feeling a bit of a prat because Dad would have told me if they'd got a dog, wouldn't he? But there's no way it's a toy.

I go in, and it still doesn't move, which is weird, because I'm right up to it now and it'd be impossible to make a toy dog look this realistic. I bend down and stroke it then I jump a mile because it's cold. And next minute I'm leaning against the wall for support for the third time today, because I've realised it's a stuffed dog. Oh, gross! Fancy having a dead dog in your room. I'm going to get a heart attack before long, living in this place.

After a bit, when my pulse has gone back to normal, I start looking round. There are loads of clothes all over the floor. Louise must have chucked her stuff in here in a big hurry. One of the bunk beds is covered in bright shiny lacy cushions, and the other one with naked Barbie dolls with sticking-out boobs. The walls are covered with posters of girl bands and the ceiling's bluey-black with stars and moons all over it. They're probably those luminous ones that shine in the dark. The books on the shelves are for quite young children.

So this is Jade's room, and now it's Louise's too. I look round. There are no hearts anywhere in sight. For some unknown reason I suddenly wonder whether Louise is sad to be surrounded by stars instead of hearts.

What a pathetic thought, Joe, you big fairy!

Right – only one room I haven't seen. I'm not sure that I want to. It's Louise's old room which is Eleanor's now. I go back to my own room and sit on the bed. Then I get up again. It's *not* my room. It's *her* room and *her* bed. It'll always be hers because I'm only a visitor, just here for six months. Dad and Sylvia had better get that straight. Dad and I are moving out on May the second. That's definite. It'll be a big relief – for Dad too. He'll never hack it with all these girls, I know he won't. It's one thing dropping in and chatting, but it's not the same as living with them and seeing their knickers all over the place and putting up with their stupid moods and everything.

Right, I think I'll go and explore downstairs now . . . But first I'll just have a quick look in Eleanor's room. Just a really quick one.

It's right next door to mine. What am I saying? It's right next door to her old one. I turn the handle, push the door open and . . . what a tip! This is worse than my room on a bad day. There are clothes and shoes everywhere and all the drawers and cupboard doors are open, and there are CDs and floppy discs on the bits of floor that aren't covered with clothes. Then there's the rug that Sylvia's chucked in here. As for the walls, they're hideous. I've never seen so many pink hearts.

'I'm going to try and get it sorted out before they get back.'

I turn round at the sound of Sylvia's voice, and go a bit red. It's like I'm snooping.

'I was just seeing where everything is – the bathroom and everything.'

She grins at me. 'My bedroom's got an en-suite shower room and there's another toilet downstairs. So don't worry – we haven't all got to share the one bathroom.' It doesn't sound like Sylvia talking. She's changed. She nods at the mess on the floor. 'Eleanor had to clear her room out in a bit of a hurry!'

I can just imagine her chucking everything on the floor in a big temper. I bet it's not that she was in a hurry, it's because she didn't want to move out of her own room. I feel a sudden twinge of guilt. If I hadn't gone on about prison cells to Louise, Eleanor could have stayed where she was and I would have gone in here. It's easy to rip down wallpaper.

I'm back on that guilty, angry merry-go-round again. It's not my fault she has to give her room up – it's the selfish adults. They ought to get their act together.

Dad, Sylvia and I eat cheese and lettuce sandwiches at the kitchen table. If only it was just us three all the time. I could hack that. Dad said Eleanor and the others go to their dad's once a fortnight. What's stopping them going *every* weekend?

Maybe I can make that happen . . . 'How often do they go to their dad's?'

'As little as possible as far as Eleanor is concerned. She finds it rather boring round there. Her dad's wife Penny has got seven-year-old twin boys, you see.'

'Eleanor's got Louise,' I point out helpfully.

'Louise is quite young for her age. She still enjoys playing with Jade, and Jamie and Max, the twins. So Eleanor feels rather out on a limb.'

Bummer!

I suddenly remember the dead dog. 'I saw a dog in the room with the bunk beds . . .'

Sylvia claps a hand to her mouth and jumps up. 'Omigod! You didn't, did you? That girl! I'll kill her when she gets back.' Then she rushes out.

'That's Buster, that is,' says Dad, grinning.

'Buster? Is he real?'

'He belonged to Sylvia's eccentric old uncle. When the old dog died, the uncle decided to have him stuffed – you know, by one of those taxidermists. And when the uncle himself died none of the relations wanted Buster. They thought it was a revolting idea. Jade overheard her mum talking about it on the phone one day. Apparently, from that moment on she wouldn't stop pestering Sylvia to let her keep the dog. She went on and on and on until Sylvia gave in.'

I'm gobsmacked. 'Jade actually wanted a stuffed dog in her bedroom?'

'She's not supposed to keep it in her room,' says Sylvia, coming back in, out of breath. 'We keep it in that glass-fronted dresser in the hall, but every so often Jade sneaks it upstairs.'

'That's Jade for you . . . completely off the wall,' says Dad. 'But I reckon you'll get on fine with her, Joe.'

'What's that supposed to mean?'

'You'll see tomorrow.'

There's a silence after he says that. I'm wishing he hadn't reminded me. I am so dreading tomorrow.

I spend the afternoon putting my stuff in my room. Half of me wants to make it look really good like my old bedroom, but the other half wants to keep it bare so everyone gets the message that I'm not planning on staying round here.

In the end I compromise and stick up two posters. There are bits of Blu-tack all over the walls, left over from where Eleanor must have had posters. I spend ages scraping it off with my nails. Not that I care about the walls being clean — I just don't want any trace of Eleanor left in here.

6 THE BEGINNING OF
   THE SENTENCE

It's weird waking up here. I don't know where I am at first. When I remember, it hits me like a bucket of icy water.

At about eleven o'clock Dad and Sylvia ask me if I want to come for a walk by the river.

Why would I want to do that?

'I'll just stay here.'

So then they keep on suggesting I get my mates over.

Oh yeah, great idea!

Then I'm back to thinking about those knickers in the bathroom.

'We won't be long,' says Sylvia. 'Make yourself at home, Joe.'

Huh!

So I'm watching telly in the sitting room, only not watching it really 'cos there's too much stuff in my head. I keep thinking I'll be going back home later. When I remember I won't, it's horrible, like homesickness.

This room looks totally neat and clean, apart from the carpet, which is mingy and worn out. There's a huge stain on it that's half hidden by the settee. Then there's a bit by the door that won't lie flat. It sticks up in a nobble. I'm thinking I might have a bash at kicking it flat, only there probably isn't any point because I expect Sylvia's tried that. Then I'm wondering why I'm having a debate about a carpet with myself. I must be cracking up.

I realise I'm starving, and think I'll raid the kitchen cupboards.

I've never seen so much food in a cupboard before. I expect we had this much when Mum was alive but I can't remember. Dad and I only ever had about one manky-looking banana and a bag of spuds with white shoots sprouting out of them. Here there are packets of mini Mars bars and KitKats, and a bumper pack of crisps and all sorts. In the fridge there's half of the flan we started yesterday, loads of different cheeses and yoghurts with big bits in them, a few sausages, a dozen eggs, some little pork pies, slices of ham . . . I don't know where to start. So I just nick one of everything, and round it off with a few more Mars bars for good measure.

I'm feeling pretty stuffed after all that, so I watch a bit more telly, play a load of guitar, watch even more telly, then get bored and think I might go out somewhere, but I'm paranoid about meeting someone I know. And that brings the whole horror story right back into sharp focus.

* * *

It's three o'clock when Dad and Sylvia get back, all bright and happy. The very sight of them makes me mad. It's OK for them, they've got exactly what they wanted. And me, I've been sentenced to six months of hell.

'We've been walking by the river,' says Dad.

What's he want? A medal?

Then Sylvia chips in, shiny-eyed, like a big kid. 'It's so beautiful!'

Anyone'd think they'd been snowboarding in the Alps.

I grunt and keep my eyes fixed on the telly, wondering how to ask my million-pound question without either of them getting the idea that I've got even a gramme of enthusiasm in me. In the end I don't have to bother.

'Ellie and the others are due back at five, Joe,' Sylvia says, in her ultra casual voice that she's brought out specially for the occasion.

I don't reply, to make sure the message comes

over loud and clear – nothing, *NOTHING* about those girls interests me one little bit.

But it really bugs me because it's impossible not to be kind of curious. Who wouldn't be? I've seen their photos all over the place and it's got me wondering whether they're planning on putting *my* photo up in the gallery too.

Just let them try.

When I get these thoughts it's like someone's given me a jab of poison and it's racing through my veins, making me sick and mad. I spend the next hour in agony, trying to think what I'm actually going to say when I see them. I know what I'm going to say to Eleanor – nothing. But Louise . . . that's a difficult one. I expect she'll probably rush up to her room and hide in her cupboard. Can't blame her. Every time I think about what happened outside the canteen I feel guilty. That person yelling at her can't have been me. It was what Dean said that made me so wild. Louise was just the poor kid who got it in the neck. Maybe I should try to be nice to her. I don't want her to be scared of me or anything.

Then there's Jade. What are you supposed to say to a weird six-year-old?

If you're planning on smuggling that dead dog into your room, can you make sure you shut the door? Cheers.

By five o'clock I've driven myself up the wall. I'm sitting in my room because it seems like the safest place to be. But then I think – no, the sitting room or the kitchen or wherever Dad and Sylvia are would be better, because if I'm in my room, I'll have to come down at some point, and that'll give *her* a big advantage in the very first round.

So I'm in the sitting room with Sylvia and Dad and they're both making pathetic conversation like their lives depend on it. It's bad enough that Sylvia's all different, but now Dad's acting strange too.

He says Jim's car is blue, and I'm taking

loads of subtle glances out of the window, dreading seeing anything blue. When it pulls up my pulse rate shoots off the scale. Technically, I'm dead.

'Here they are!' says Sylvia, jumping up and going to the door. Dad gets up too and just stands there. I go and stand next to him because I'm suddenly petrified he might go out and leave me here. He rubs his hands like we're about to settle down to watch England playing in the World Cup. If only.

Then I get this flashback of something that happened about three weeks after Mum died, when Dad and I watched a Cup Final match on telly together. He rubbed his hands just like he's doing now. I can remember it like it was yesterday – they way he'd pulled out all the stops to make it really good because we were both feeling rubbish. He'd ordered a pizza to be delivered to our door. I'd only ever seen that happen on telly. It was absolutely whopping, and while we scoffed it Dad drank beer and I drank Coke, then he got this posh ice cream out of the freezer. Mum had bought it before she died. She'd said we must keep it for a special occasion. So when we were eating it in front of the Cup Final we were both thinking about Mum saying that, but neither of us wanted to mention it. I remember the lump in my throat was so big I could hardly swallow the ice cream.

And now here I am, getting these flashbacks and feeling that lump again, even though I haven't felt sad about Mum for ages. I'm looking through the window and I can see them piling out of the car. What pants timing!

'They're excited,' Dad says, putting his hand on my shoulder.

He's trying to make it a dead casual gesture, but it's not coming off. I just want to go home – back to our other house, our real home, just him and me. But I can't. I'm trapped. There's no way out.

Sylvia's opening the front door. Eleanor's saying 'bye to her dad at the car, looking completely hacked off. The other two are belting up the drive.

'Is he here?' calls out the little one. So this is Jade.

'Yes, come and say hello.'

And I stand there with Dad's hand still on my shoulder, and the kid comes careering into the room and trips over the bit of rucked-up carpet, crashing straight into me, and I'm doubled over in agony because she got me where it really hurts. She's in a heap on the floor at my feet, but she doesn't realise I'm bent double because she shoots up, head-butting me on the way, and she's got the hardest head known to man, which means *she* can't feel a thing but I'm a wreck, throbbing and sweating and trying not to look like a wimp.

And when I finally stop seeing stars I realise Louise is standing in the hall staring at me like

I'm a freak show. For a moment nobody moves, and I suddenly totally understand what the expression 'suspended in time' means.

Then Sylvia kind of breaks the spell. She dives forward, grabs Jade's hand and lugs her back.

'What do you say?' she demands in this sort of bewildered whine. 'You've really hurt poor Joe.'

A puzzled look covers Jade's face and she looks round the room, as though she might see some kind of clue about how she could possibly have hurt me.

'Sorry,' she says eventually.

' 's OK,' I tell her, trying for something resembling a smile, because the kid's all worried now.

Then *she* appears.

'Here's Ellie!' smiles Sylvia, because no one else is speaking.

For a split second my eyes meet hers by mistake, then she turns and goes off upstairs.

Dad coughs and rubs his hands together again. Sylvia says, 'What about a cup of tea and some lovely doughnuts?'

'Doesn't Ellie like Joe?' says Jade.

'Course she does!' laughs Sylvia. She's sounding pretty hysterical.

Dad's hand falls away from my shoulder.

My sentence has begun.

7 POP, RAP AND WAR

'Doughnuts! My favourite.'

Oh yeah, Dad? First I knew about it.

And as the happy couple go off to the kitchen I see a streak of lightning in the hall out of the corner of my eye. That's Louise diving in to join them.

I'm expecting Jade to follow but she climbs up on to the arm of the sofa and sticks out one leg.

'Can *you* do this, Joe?'

'Nope.'

'Are you coming down for a doughnut,

Ellie?' comes Sylvia's bright voice from the hall.

I'm thinking I'd better get into the kitchen quick before *she* does, but Jade's got other plans.

'Can you do *this* then?' She's jumped off the sofa and now she's curling her top lip up at the corner.

I can, but I'm not about to show her. It's embarrassing.

'D'you fancy a doughnut, Jade?'

'D'you know what I call Ellie?'

She obviously doesn't believe in answering questions.

'What?'

She's still balanced on one leg, staring straight ahead. 'Smelly.'

I smirk. Maybe the kid's going to turn out to be OK.

'It's a good rhyme, isn't it?'

'Wicked.'

I turn to go.

'Do you want to see Buster?'

'I've seen him.'

'He's dead.'

'I know.'

'D'you want to talk to him?'

'*What?*'

She grabs my hand. 'It's better than eating doughnuts.'

I don't know what she's on about but I'm getting yanked upstairs, and guess who's coming down?

'Stop!' screeches Jade, putting both hands up like a policeman. 'It's bad luck to cross on the stairs.'

'You go back then,' says Eleanor, carrying on walking.

And next minute I'm staggering around in the hall because Jade has shoved me backwards with such force. I'm quite impressed with her strength, considering she's only a thin little kid. All the same I feel a right idiot, especially when I see Eleanor smirking as she goes past.

When we get to the top of the stairs, Jade flings open her bedroom door, whizzes round the room touching everything that's hers and saying, 'That's mine . . . that's mine . . . mine, mine, mine, mine . . .'

'So yours is the top bunk with the . . . naked dolls?'

But she's looking round with her hands on her hips like a grown up. 'Where's he gone?'

'Oh yeah – I forgot. Your mum put him back in the case downstairs.'

She catapults out of the door. 'Come on, Joe!'

'What about a doughnut?' calls Sylvia from the kitchen when she hears us crashing downstairs.

'Joe wants to see Buster,' Jade tells her.

'I think Joe can answer for himself actually, Jade.'

I suppose I'd better get it over with. 'Yeah, come on, Jade. Aren't you hungry?'

It's pointless asking Jade questions. She never answers them. She just grabs my hand and walks me into the kitchen. It's weird but I get another flashback to when Mum was alive. Why does it keep happening all of a sudden? This time I'm remembering when I didn't want to go to someone's birthday party. Most of the other kids went flying in through the front door and didn't even bother to turn round to say 'bye to their mums, they were so excited. But I wouldn't let go of Mum's hand and she had to take me right into the sitting room where all the other kids were sitting round in a circle on the floor watching the birthday boy open his presents.

So we walk into the kitchen, Jade and me, and I'm half expecting to hear a voice saying, 'Go on, Joe, give your present to Harry.'

Eleanor and Louise are both silently chewing, studying their plates. Dad's grinning at me, and Sylvia's telling Jade that I'm perfectly capable of walking to the table on my own.

Little does she know.

'This is where Louise normally sits,' Jade

informs me, 'only we've all squashed up so you can fit in too, now you're in our family.'

I cringe at the sound of that word. She's pointing to the chair between Eleanor and Dad. No way am I going to sit there. There are two other spare chairs on the other side of Dad. 'I'll sit here,' I mumble, going for the chair next to Dad's.

'No, you can't sit there. That's Mum's place.'

'It doesn't matter,' says Sylvia brightly from over by the kettle.

'Yes it does,' says Jade. 'You've already had to squash up to fit Nick in.'

There's a snigger from Eleanor, then she nudges Louise and tries to get her to smile. Louise is still staring at her plate. Her cheeks look fatter than ever because she's taken such a whopping mouthful of doughnut.

'You can sit in my place,' says Jade. 'I don't mind sitting next to Smelly.'

Eleanor glares at her sister. Louise stuffs the

whole of the rest of her doughnut in.

The chair Jade's sorted out for me is next to Louise. It scrapes on the floor when I pull it back to get in, and she jumps a mile.

'There you go!' says Sylvia, putting a teapot on the mat in the middle of the table. She pours out a cup for me. 'Help yourself to sugar, Joe.'

But I daren't. My hand's trembling. I'll only spill it all over the table.

Dad offers me a doughnut. I take it. God knows how I'm going to eat it.

'Can I go up to my room, Mum?' says Eleanor. 'I've got to sort out my stuff.' Her voice is hard as nails.

'Yes, off you go, love,' says Sylvia brightly.

'Can Louise help?' says Eleanor.

We all look at Louise. She can't talk, her mouth's so full of doughnut. Maybe she planned it that way.

'Course she can.'

Louise gets up.

'Finish your mouthful first,' says Sylvia.

So then the poor kid flops back down again and starts chewing for England. She's panicking because Eleanor's gone and *she's* still stuck there next to Ogre Joe.

I make a decision. I'm going to be nice to her, get her to see that I'm not horrible really. I'm going to start right now while Eleanor's not here to sneer.

'D'you want some more tea?' I'm holding the teapot right over her cup all ready to pour.

She chews even faster and shakes her head hard.

Maybe I'll try a joke. 'It's not got arsenic in it, you know.'

I grin round. Sylvia and Dad look quite pleased with my effort. Jade's doing a finger-painting on her plate with the jam from her doughnut.

'Can I go now, Mum?' says Louise in the smallest voice in the world.

Sylvia nods and Louise nearly knocks her chair over she's so keen to get out.

Well, that worked well, I thought. Not.

After tea I go up to my room and shut the door firmly. I can hear all sorts of noises from next door where Eleanor and Louise are tidying Eleanor's new room. Time for a bit of showing off on the guitar, I think. Might make Eleanor think again before she goes rubbishing me to Kelly Grey. I open my Beatles book and start with *Yellow Submarine* as that's easy.

But I've only played about two lines when the sound of Kylie comes through the wall. Eleanor's deliberately drowning me out with the top twenty. Well, two can play at that game. I switch on the radio bit of my pathetically ancient ghetto blaster and turn the volume right up. Then I realise that's not getting back at her at all. All I'm doing is listening to the same programme as her on Radio One – only she's probably got miles better reception than me.

Right. This means war. I twiddle about with the tuning knob, trying to find something loud enough. I stop when I get to a station playing rap. This should do it. I turn the volume knob as far round as it will go.

The next song they play is rock. I get my guitar and start leaping about, pretending I'm playing. It feels really good. I'm imagining I'm on a stage with thousands of screaming fans in the audience. I open the wardrobe door because there's a mirror in there, so now I can really imagine myself on that stage.

But then I see something reflected in the mirror. Something behind me. I swing round and there's Jade standing in the doorway, her hands over her ears. Sylvia's next to her, and just behind them is Eleanor, with horrible mocking eyes.

'I *did* knock,' says Sylvia, looking almost as embarrassed as me, 'but you didn't hear.'

I stand there like a prat, because I don't know what to do – although killing Eleanor is pretty high up on the list.

'Can you turn it down a bit, Joe?'

So I do. Then it's even more embarrassing.

'My eardrums was bursting,' says Jade, letting her hands flop to her side. 'Were you pretending to be a pop star?'

Why don't they all just go?

'*Were* you?' asks Eleanor.

I'm just about to tell her where to get off when Sylvia turns round and shoos them both off, then follows herself. 'Show me how you're getting on with your room, Ellie.'

Jade pops her head round her mum. 'D'you want to help, Joe? And I'll ask Nick if he wants to. Then the whole family will be in Ellie's room.'

'Joe's got enough to do,' says Sylvia briskly.

'Yeah, he's got to practise for his Albert Hall appearance next week,' Eleanor comments sarcastically.

I kick the door shut and flop on my bed.
How am I going to bear six months of *this*?

8 YESTERDAY

My eyes open. My brain starts to tick over. I sit bolt upright in bed. I remember where I am and feel sick.

Seven thirty-five a.m. I get out of bed and open my door as quietly as possible. I don't see anyone, but I can hear loads of voices close by. I shut the door and lean against it, terrified. I can't go out there. There are girls. I don't want them to see me in my boxers.

If I can just make it to the bathroom . . .

I open my door again – about ten centimetres. Not a sound. I peer out on to the landing. No one. I creep to the bathroom door and turn the handle.

'Go away. I'm doing a poo. I'll be ages.'

Doesn't Jade care what she says to anyone?

Sylvia comes flying out of her bedroom, fully dressed. 'Use our bathroom, Joe. We've finished in there.' She hardly looks at me, just belts off downstairs.

I want to ask her where the other two are and where Dad is, but I'm too late. My brain's never been that quick in the mornings.

'Sorry about the smell.' Jade is walking across the landing, holding her nose. She's wearing inside-out pyjama bottoms and a fluffy jumper.

I bolt into the bathroom and lock the door. That's when I realise I've left my toothbrush in my room. There's hardly any toothpaste in the tube but I squeeze a bit on to my finger and hope for the best. A few minutes later I'm ready for the return journey. I open the door the regulation ten centimetres. Again there's no one around so I plunge out on to the landing and make a dive for my room. I'm in the nick of time because there are footsteps on the stairs. I don't hang about to see who it is.

When I get downstairs, Jade and Louise are sitting at the table eating toast and jam. Eleanor's leaning against the dishwasher with a bowl of something or other. Sylvia's racing around with armloads of washing and Dad's pouring boiling water into six mugs.

'Tea, Joe?'

'Yes please.'

'Help yourself to cereal or whatever,' says Sylvia. 'It's a free-for-all in the mornings.'

The cereal packet's on the draining board but there aren't any bowls left in the cupboard, so I'm not sure what to do. Dad's gone outside to put washing on the line, Jade's talking loudly to herself about cats having baby kittens, Louise is showing deep interest in her toast, Sylvia's gone upstairs now. There's only Eleanor left to ask.

No fear.

Luckily Dad comes in at that moment.

'Where are the bowls, Dad?'

'You'll have to get one out of the dishwasher and wash it up.'

How can *I with her there?*

She doesn't make any attempt to move.

Dad realises I'm in a bit of a fix. 'I'll do it. You unload the rest of the clothes from the washing machine into this basket.'

The kitchen's in an L shape. The bottom of the L is where the washing machine is. I start dragging things out of it, and my fingers come across something that feels like a piece of raw liver. I look at what I'm holding. It's some globby stuff inside a bra. Ugh! Yuk! I quickly let go and pull out everything else then belt back into the kitchen. 'Done it.'

'Are you doing clubs after school like Eleanor and Louise, Joe?' asks Sylvia, coming back in at a hundred miles an hour.

I'm still shaking from the bra experience. I gulp. 'I thought I'd just come home on the bus same as usual.'

'OK. That's fine. The key's in the bottom of the mat outside the back door. I'm at work today and I'll be back with the troops at about half five. Will you be all right on your own?'

You're not kidding. I can't wait to be on my own.

'Did you see *The Grotes* last night?' asks Dean.

'Yeah, wicked,' says Andy. 'What about the bit where Mac punctures Tanya's gel bra!'

Thank God my head's down so they can't see my face. I'm the one scribbling up the French this week, but it's no good, I can't concentrate. Andy mentioning that 'b' word has got me remembering how awful it was when my fingers felt it.

' 'spect Joe was watching a match, weren't you?' Jack says, punching my shoulder and making my pen go right across the page.

'Look what you've made me do!'

Like they cared. 'Come on, Joe, what'd you watch?'

'I was playing my guitar.'

'Coming, Joe?'

It's morning break. Chris Counter's standing in the doorway of our classroom.

I'm not expecting him. 'Thought it was after lunch. Hang on.' I go to the walk-in cupboard to collect my guitar, wondering who's going to take the mick first, Jack or Dean (Andy's in the toilet).

'Have fun with Kate Moss!' (It's Jack.)

Chris looks a bit puzzled but doesn't say anything.

I don't know if I'm looking worried, but he tries to be extra friendly and chatty as we're walking along the corridor.

'Thanks for joining, by the way. You should have heard me on the piano. I sounded terrible.'

He grins as he pushes open the music room door. I follow him in, feeling my palms getting sweaty. I've just realised I never even asked what song they're playing.

Eleanor and the other two are messing about on Chris's drum kit. They all look up. Eleanor looks straight back down again.

Chris hits everyone with a radiant beam and a big announcer's voice. 'Say hello to our new guitarist!'

My face starts to go red. I should never have agreed to joining the band. There's too much stuff going on here – Kelly Grey fancying me, Eleanor hating my guts, me feeling nervous about playing guitar in front of her . . . Well, let's face it, I'm not used to playing in front of anyone, but I've picked a right bunch for my first public appearance, haven't I?

Eleanor's pretending she's got some kind of massive interest in drum kits all of a sudden.

Kelly rushes up and grabs my shoulders. 'You're such a saviour, Joe!'

'Can you play any Beatles songs, Joe?' asks Vicky, the year-nine girl.

Beatles? Cool! It's like hearing that an exam's been cancelled. 'Yeah, sure. Which one?' I drawl.

'*Yesterday,*' says Chris.

My eyes meet Eleanor's. She's caught me with my defences down and she's wearing a challenging look.

I look as casual as possible. 'Yeah. No problem. I'll just have to have a few goes – you know – on my own . . .'

Like about a hundred.

'You don't want to try it now then?'

'Nah. I'll leave it till next time.'

'Shall we have a run-through without Joe to show him how we're doing it?' pipes up Kelly.

Eleanor looks up. 'Let's wait till . . .' She can't even say my name.

'Wait till Joe's got it sorted?' Chris finishes

off for her. 'Yeah, I agree. We've still got time.'

Want a bet? It's going to be impossible to practise with her *around.*

9 TALKING ABOUT TELLY

The front door key is inside the bottom of Sylvia's doormat. It's taken me ages to find it. I could have sworn Sylvia said it was *under* the doormat, but I couldn't find it so I looked under every possible thing round the front and the back and the side of the house. Then I came back to the doormat and looked again, only this time I chucked it down in disgust, I was feeling that hacked off, and something clunked against the doorstep. That's when I discovered it. And that's when I remembered that Sylvia did actually say *in* the doormat. There's a ripped bit – you have to put your hand right inside to get it.

What a waste of time. I've only got till half-past five before Sylvia gets back with the others. I look at my watch. Forty minutes to get started on *Yesterday*. I go crashing up to my room and grab my Beatles songbook. It's on page fifty-four and it looks awful. I'll never crack this by Friday. It'd be like trying to learn Hebrew. I'm just going to have to get out of it somehow. But then this picture comes flashing up in my mind of that patronising smirk on Eleanor's face, and I know there's no way I can pull out now.

The strings on my guitar feel a bit floppy and they sound terrible. Great! Jade must have sneaked in and twiddled a few of the tuning knobs when I was in the bathroom or something. Now I've got to spend ages getting it tuned and I've never been any good at that. I'm going to go spare with that kid when she gets back. Only not in front of Eleanor. No way must she find out that I'm rattled.

So I've hardly cracked the first line when I hear the front door opening. I look at my watch. Five thirty-five. Where did that time go? Someone's belting upstairs. Bet I can guess who.

'I thought I'd find you in here!' Jade's standing in my doorway, grinning her head off.

'Let's get one thing straight,' I tell her, glaring hard. 'You don't come in my room when I'm not here and you definitely don't touch my stuff, especially my guitar. Got it?'

She looks like she's working on some clever line of defence when Eleanor's superior voice comes ringing out from downstairs. 'Don't worry, Jade, he's only in a bad mood because he's got so much guitar practice to do.'

'Practice? Why?' Jade calls back, still looking at me.

'Because he's playing in our band for the Children in Need concert.'

'Ooh! That's nice!' comes Sylvia's singsong

voice. It sounds like she's on her way upstairs.

'Can *we* go to the concert, Mum?' Jade asks.

'I think it's in school time, isn't it, Joe?'

She's standing in the doorway too.

'Yeah.'

'But it's lovely that you and Ellie are in the band together, Joe. She's just getting something to eat, then I'll send her up to practise with you.'

What? 'No!'

I didn't mean it to come out quite so fast and loud. Sylvia looks a bit embarrassed and goes off mumbling about tea, dragging Jade with her. So now I've got to practise really quietly to make sure *she* doesn't hear.

After about five minutes there's a faint knock on my door.

I go for a gruff voice, just in case it's Eleanor. 'Who is it?'

No answer. I open the door. The landing's empty.

Oh, *I* get it. 'Yes, very amusing,' I say in a

loud, bored voice. 'You can come out now, Jade.'

Still no reply. I go into her room. No sign of her. The room's right above the kitchen. I can hear her talking loudly down there. That's odd. I know Sylvia's in the kitchen too and Dad's not back yet, so that leaves Eleanor and Louise. Surely Eleanor wouldn't play a juvenile game like that?

Back in my room I can't concentrate. I didn't imagine that knock on my door, I know I didn't. Then just when I'm getting back into my guitar, there it is again. This time I yank the door open immediately. Louise is standing there, looking petrified.

'Mum says do you want a cup of tea?' Her eyes are on the carpet.

I try for a big friendly smile so's not to frighten her away again. 'Great! I'll come and get it.'

' 's OK, I'll bring it.' She turns to go.

'Louise?'

She turns back, all big-eyed.

'Look, I'm sorry I sounded off at you the other day. I was just upset.' She bites her lip and I keep going. 'It was really nice of you to offer me your room.'

' 's OK.'

Then we're both stuck so I give her a sort of nod and she races off.

I'm wondering if she'll tell Eleanor what I said. And what if she does? Will it make any difference to anything? And do I care if it does?

My head's rattling with questions. I don't know any of the answers. All I know is that the atmosphere in this place is terrible.

It's nearly seven when Dad gets back. Jade's had her tea ages ago but I said I'd rather wait for Dad. I didn't know Eleanor and Louise had said they'd wait too, so we're all sitting round the kitchen table. Jade is supposed to be getting ready for bed but Sylvia's forgotten about her and she's galloping from side to side near the sink. Then she suddenly stops and watches Dad chewing.

'It's nice having a boy and a man, isn't it?'

I feel like I'm an interesting museum piece. Eleanor gives Jade a *dur* look and Sylvia starts gabbling.

'Joe and Eleanor are in a band together, Nick. Great, isn't it?'

'Nice one!' says Dad. I can tell he isn't concentrating. Knowing Dad, I expect he's thinking that if he really wolfs it down he'll be in time to see the match that kicks off at seven-thirty.

'Clean your teeth, Jade,' says Sylvia. 'I'll be up in a minute.'

But Jade's in a daydream. She sits down at the table and says, 'You know Buster?

'Uh-huh.'

'You know he's dead?'

'Uh-huh.'

'So that means we haven't actually got any pets, have we – I mean ones what are alive?'

Sylvia narrows her eyes. 'No . . .'

'Well, I was wondering if we could have one. You know – an alive one. Like a kitten . . .'

'What made you suddenly think about that?'

'Yeah, let's get a kitten,' says Eleanor, looking happy about something for a change. 'That would be brilliant.'

Jade knits her eyebrows together crossly. ''Scuse me, Ellie . . .'

'What?'

'The kitten will be *mine*, remember, because I thought of it first.'

'Hang on a sec,' says Sylvia. 'It's not a good idea, you know. I mean, there'd be arguments about who's allowed to feed it and who's allowed to . . .' She's looking at Dad for help. 'What else do kittens do, Nick?'

'They do their own thing, don't they? I

mean, there's no need to take them for walks or anything like that.'

Jade smiles at him, like a teacher talking to a pupil who's just given the right answer. 'Quite right, Nick. Only you *do* have to name them, you know. But don't worry . . .' *Like we were worried*! '. . . I've already chosen a name to go with its beautiful black fur.'

Louise looks up. '*What* beautiful black fur?'

So then Jade gives us the punch line. 'You see, Lily's got three kittens to get rid of. Her cat had seven and they've only got rid of four so far.'

I'm not following this. 'Who's Lily?'

'That leaves *three*,' Jade tells me, like I'm a moron who asks the wrong questions.

'Jade went home with Lily Farrow after school . . .' Sylvia starts to fill me in.

'And she says I can come again on Thursday,' interrupts Jade, 'because we like playing with her kittens.'

'No, you're coming straight home after school

on Thursday,' Sylvia says firmly, 'otherwise Rosie doesn't have anyone to play with.'

I haven't got the faintest clue what they're on about, but I don't like the sound of Thursday one little bit. I thought I'd got that after-school time to myself.

'Don't you have to work on Thursday?' I ask Sylvia, as casually as possible.

'She does job share,' Jade explains importantly. 'She works Mondays, Tuesdays and Wednesdays, and I go to the Andersons' house after school – except today when I got invited to Lily's. Then on Thursdays and Fridays Mum looks after Rosie Anderson after school because her mum works in a big office.'

This is getting worse. Thursdays *and* Fridays. I hope that doesn't mean that Eleanor and Louise come home on the bus those days.

'So can I phone Lily and tell her we'll have Telly, Mum?'

Sylvia tips her head on one side. She does

that a lot, I've noticed. 'What are you talking about, Jade?'

'I'm calling the kitten *Telly* because that's the blackest thing in the house. I've checked. So can I phone Lily?'

'Nick and I will have a talk about it,' says Sylvia.

Dad's already nodding away. 'Fine by me.'

'Hey, cool!' says Eleanor. 'Can we have two?'

'Can we have three?' Louise seems to have lost her shyness at last.

'Any advance on three?' says Dad, looking at me.

I roll my eyes at him. Like I care.

Sylvia's getting a bit stressy. 'Hold it right there! We're deciding about *one* kitten, and one kitten only. But we're definitely not having it if there's going to be arguments.'

The three of them sit up straight all of a sudden. It reminds me of primary school when the bell for break goes and the teacher says,

'Right, let's see which table is going out first today!'

'What about you, Joe? What do *you* think?'

I couldn't care less as long as it isn't deadly shy, nasty and cold or completely crazy. 'Don't mind.'

Jade grabs her mum's hand dramatically and closes her eyes tightly, with her shoulders all hunched up, like she'll burst if she doesn't get the answer she wants. 'So can I phone Lily then?'

'Hang on a sec, Jade. Let's not go rushing in. I'll have a word with her mum. I can't pick it up until the weekend, you know . . .'

Jade's counting on her fingers.

'Five more days,' Eleanor tells her.

Sylvia's frowning at the floor. When she speaks it's obvious she's a bit nervous. 'And it'll be a lovely surprise for when you get back from Dad's.'

Eleanor explodes. 'What are we going there again for?' She flings a daggers look in my direction then turns on Sylvia again. 'I thought

Dad was supposed to be having some long-lost visitors to stay?'

Sylvia bites her lip. 'They've cancelled.'

Eleanor's really mad. 'Well, *I'm* not going, I'll tell you now!'

Time to make a quick exit, Joe.

I sneak out without a sound. But I've hardly got my foot on the bottom stair when Eleanor's voice screams out, 'No, Mum! I refuse, and that's that. You can't make me!'

10 FIGHTING FOR SPACE

I sprint up to my room. I can guess what's coming next – there we go! Crash! Bang! Thump thump thump! That girl really has got a temper. What's the betting she's going to slam the bedroom door as well?

Yep.

Still, at least I can watch the match in peace. So I'm just about to go downstairs when I hear someone coming up. Whoever it is knocks on Eleanor's door, and a second later the door opens.

'I know you're not happy about the weekend, love,' comes Sylvia's voice, all gentle, 'but Joe needs some space. He's had a big adjustment to make.'

She's left the door open so I open mine about ten centimetres to earwig better. I expect they think I'm downstairs watching telly.

'What about *me*? Don't you think I've had a pretty big adjustment to make?'

'Yes, but not as big as Joe's. He's come from a quiet set-up with one other male person to a crazy set-up with four females.'

Eleanor's getting sweaty. 'Come off it, Mum. He's getting everything he wants – *my* room for a start! This whole deal is so unfair!'

'Hold on a sec, Eleanor. Joe's had to make sacrifices too.'

'Yeah? Like what?'

'Like privacy.'

'Yeah, well I've lost my privacy too. I tell you, Mum, he's horrible to me . . .' *Yeah, right, blame it all on me.* 'I can't stick his guts.'

'Ssh! He might hear you.'

'I don't care if he does.'

'Oh Eleanor. Think about it from his point of view. He's got to fit into a routine with a load of girls who probably scare him stiff. And it's *your* house, not his. He must feel a real outsider at times. He's given up so much freedom, Ellie.'

Eleanor sounds like sarcasm on legs. 'So you thought you'd give him back a couple of days of his precious freedom at the weekend, did you? Poor old Joe! Let him have everything he wants. Never mind us lot. Parcel us up and send us off to Dad's. We're not important.'

She's really winding me up now. She ought to realise I don't have any choice either. I didn't ask to come and live here. I feel like banging on the wall and telling her where to get off.

'Don't be unreasonable, Eleanor. *You* get to have a break from *Joe* as well, don't you?'

Eleanor's in a real stress. 'Why does it

have to be *us* who go? Why can't you send *him* away?'

My blood hits boiling point. I yank open my door and go barging into her room, fixing her with a big evil. 'So where d'you think I ought to go then? My mum's?'

Sylvia gasps, Eleanor's eyes go wide and they both freeze in that position. Then Eleanor turns her back on me, Sylvia pats me on the shoulder and Jade walks in. This kid really does choose her moments.

'I thought your mum was dead, Joe?'

Sylvia breathes in sharply as though she's banged her elbow or something, then she shoos Jade out of the room, flapping her hand and looking frazzled. 'Go and see what the others are doing please, Jade.'

Jade must think that if she whispers, it's OK. 'Yes, but is she dead or not?'

'Oh shut up!' screams Eleanor, still with her back to everyone.

I reckon it's time for another one of my quick exits. 'I'm going to watch the match with Dad.'

Jade follows me. I can hear her footsteps pattering really softly behind me.

'Joe?'

We're at the bottom of the stairs. 'Uh-huh?'

'D'you think your mum and Buster know each other in heaven?'

I don't like thinking about Mum in heaven. I'd rather just keep thinking about how she was when she was alive.

'Doubt it.'

'Why? Do you mean that heaven's too big for everyone to know each other, or do you think your mum didn't want to make friends with Buster?'

All this stuff about heaven. I don't know what I'm supposed to say to a six-year-old.

'I've no idea, and I'm going to watch the match now, OK?' I push open the sitting-room door.

'I'll go and ask Buster then . . .' *She's clearly completely loony.* 'Oh, by the way, what does your mum look like, then I can describe her to Buster properly?'

Why can't she just leave it alone?

'She's . . . I dunno . . . like an ordinary mother . . .'

Jade's standing there, waiting for me to say more, but I can't. It's screwing me up. So I shut the door in her face and sit down next to Dad.

He's leaning forward, protesting to the telly. 'Oh come on! Referee!'

Back to normality. That's better.

This week is doing my head in. I'm hacked off with everyone, even Dad. In fact mainly Dad. He's changed just as much as Sylvia since we've been here. It's like he's trying to be everyone's best friend.

'Can you fix my lampshade, Nick?'

'Course I can! They don't say "Nick's a fixer"

for nothing, you know, Louise.'

'Nick, can you take me over to Tasha's?'

'No probs, Ellie. Van or car?'

'Watch me, Nick. Bet you can't do this!' That's Jade swinging backwards and forwards on her hands, like a frog, with her back legs wrapped round her arms.

'Wow! Skilful! You'll have to teach me how to do that!'

But it seems like he's forgotten about me.

'Dad, can you give me a lift on Saturday? We've got an away match.'

'Er . . .' (turning to Sylvia), 'what are we doing on Saturday, Sylv?'

She looks frazzled. 'Off the top of my head, about a million things.'

Dad puts on the same expression and I feel like some demanding kid who's getting on the grown-ups' nerves. 'I expect we'll sort something out, Joe.'

Cheers, Dad. Don't suppose you're interested in

watching me play in the match? Oh no, silly question. You only do girly things now, don't you?

11 FULL ON

On Friday after lunch I go along to the big music room with my guitar. I'm nervous. I can play *Yesterday*, but only just.

'Great!' says Chris. 'Let's get started.'

Eleanor's looking kind of sulky and fierce at the same time. She's leaning against the piano. I wonder if she has to arrange her face like this whenever she knows I'm going to appear.

Kelly suddenly starts jumping up and down and talking in a high-pitched girly voice. 'Chris, I hope you don't mind me making a little suggestion, do you?'

Chris shakes his head.

'Well, I had an idea. You know how we couldn't decide who was going to take the lead, me or Ellie?'

'Yeah . . .'

That's funny. I thought Kelly said she was the lead.

'Well, why don't we let Joe decide?' Kelly smiles round at everyone like she's waiting for a round of applause.

'S'pose it makes sense,' says Vicky, fiddling around on the piano.

Chris turns to me. 'That OK with you, Joe?'

Eleanor's giving me one of her hard looks.

Right, Eleanor Stern, so you think I'm useless on guitar, do you? Let's see what you're like at singing, shall we?

'Yeah, fine,' I drawl.

'D'you want me to go first, Ell?' says Kelly, all smiles.

Eleanor shrugs.

'I'll play the chords on the piano,' says Chris. 'It'll be a bit rough but it's just so you can hear their voices, Joe.'

Eleanor grabs a copy of the song and stands next to Vicky, ready to do the backing for Kelly. The song sheet's shaking. She's nervous. Good. Serves her right.

Chris takes charge. 'OK, so this is Kelly on lead, Joe, and the other two on backing.' He plays the intro and Kelly sways from side to side with her eyes closed. *Who does she think she is? Madonna?*

'This bit's you on the guitar,' Chris tells me. I nod.

A breathy warbly voice comes out of Kelly's mouth. It makes Vicky and Eleanor sound really ordinary in the background. Chris goes a bit louder for the second verse. Kelly opens her eyes and stares into the distance like she's in Wembley Arena. Then she lets rip, belting out the lyrics all passionate and strong.

It's good in one way, because she's so loud and confident. But it's also pretty embarrassing. Chris is raising his eyebrows at me. 'That enough?' he mouths.

I nod.

'Right, Ellie, your turn.'

Kelly stops dramatically, smiles round and swaps place with Eleanor. This is going to be interesting. 'Give us the music, Ell,' says Kelly. 'I don't know the backing bits by heart, you know.'

Eleanor hands it across. She doesn't know where to look now she's not got the music so she fixes her eyes on the wall. She's gone all pink at the tops of her cheeks.

Chris begins playing.

Eleanor should be singing by now. But she's dropped her head. Chris repeats the introduction. 'OK, Eleanor?'

She looks up and nods. Then she starts. Her voice isn't very loud, but it's good. Miles better than Kelly's. I've got the feeling Kelly's watching me. I turn my head to see. I'm right. She flashes me one of her embarrassing smiles. I ignore it and look back at Eleanor. But she's stopped singing, and she's staring at me coldly.

Chris stops playing. He's looking puzzled. 'Wh-what do you think, Joe?'

I think I'm wishing I'd never agreed to make this decision.

Vicky's standing by the window, texting someone. 'I reckon Kelly's a bit loud,' she says without bothering to look up.

'Well, it's good to sound confident,' I say.

Kelly flashes me another one of those hideous smiles. If I decide on *her* she'll think I fancy her . . .

But I'm not going for Eleanor. No way. Not after the way she's treated me.

So it'll *have* to be Kelly.

'Eleanor's a bit quiet though, isn't she, Joe?'

says Vicky, waving to someone through the window now.

'Yeah . . .'

Then Eleanor suddenly speaks. It's obvious she's hacked off. 'Go with Kelly. That's fine. I'd rather do backing anyway.'

'Are you sure?' says Chris, frowning.

'Yeah, positive.'

'Right, that's settled,' says Vicky. 'Let's get on with it.'

Kelly puts her hands up to her mouth and makes her eyes go really big. 'I'm the *lead*! Omigod!'

What a prima donna.

Eleanor's got that hard look on her face again. Chris is frowning.

'Let's do it properly with guitar and drums and everything,' smiles Kelly. (She's so up herself.)

Chris looks a bit shell-shocked. 'OK then. Let's try it . . .'

I'm quite nervous about the guitar but I keep

my eyes glued to the music all through, and it comes off all right. Not brilliant, just all right. I could do with new strings really. I've had these ones ages.

'Great!' says Chris when we've finished.

We all know it's not though – well, all except Kelly.

'It sounds boring,' says Vicky. Then she looks at me and starts gabbling. 'Oh, I didn't mean because of you or anything, Joe. The guitar's cool.'

'I ought to get new strings . . .'

'No, it's great. So's the drums.' She frowns. 'It's just kind of . . . boring, isn't it?'

Eleanor and I both nod, then realise we're agreeing and quickly stop.

'Let's have another go,' says Chris.

So we do. But it's no better.

Vicky's phone rings and she walks across the room and starts talking to whoever's on the other end.

Chris looks round the rest of us. 'How about we all practise over the weekend then meet up on Monday?'

'Fine by me,' grins Kelly. 'I know mine anyway.'

Eleanor shrugs again.

I nod.

'OK, Monday, same time,' says Chris, putting his drumsticks away.

'Seeya!' says Vicky, rushing off with her phone clamped to her ear.

Kelly comes right up to me and starts stroking my guitar.

I've got to get out of here. 'OK, see you Monday then.'

But just before I turn to go I catch a glimpse of Eleanor's face. The hard look's completely gone. It's like she's packed all her feelings into her eyes and turned them full on.

It's weird. She got me rattled when she went off on one last night and now she's got me rattled again. Only this time I don't feel like yelling at her. I just feel . . . wrong inside.

12 PEELING BACK THE LAYERS

'What's up with you, Joe?' It's Jack, prodding me from across the aisle.

I can't stop picturing Eleanor's face during that rehearsal. 'Nothing.'

'Well, what are you staring out the window for?'

'Just thinking.'

'What about?'

'I'm thinking I'd better get three new strings for my guitar.'

'Why? Have they bust?'

'No, just don't sound great.'

'I thought guitars had six strings.'

'Can't afford six. Can't afford three either. Might settle for one.'

Louise and Eleanor are on the bus too, near the front. Yesterday Louise went to her friend's house and Eleanor was in a netball match. So today'll be the first time we all get off the bus together. It's going to be the pits. There's no way I'm walking home with them.

Dean clicks his fingers in front of my face. 'Joe! Get back to planet earth. The spacecraft's about to arrive at your stop. You getting off, or what?'

I blink.

'I'll come into town with you if you want,' he goes on.

'Eh?'

'To get your guitar string.'

'Trouble is, I don't have much money on me.'

'We'll stop off at my place and I'll get Mum

to shell out. She won't mind as long as she gets it back.'

The bus is pulling up. Eleanor and Louise get off.

'Say 'bye-bye to your stepsisters, then,' says Andy, grinning.

'They're *not* my stepsisters!' I hiss at him.

The bus pulls away. Louise is on the pavement smiling and waving at someone. I crane my neck and press my face against the window. I can see Sylvia and Jade approaching. Eleanor's not waving. She's just staring like she's in a trance. I wonder what she's thinking about.

Andy's really getting on my nerves. 'If they're not your stepsisters, what are they then?'

I ignore him.

'So when do we get to come over to your house?' he goes on. 'I want to see what it's like.'

'It's only 'cos he fancies Eleanor so much,' says Jack, grinning.

'No I don't! *You* do.'

'Who wouldn't? She's the fittest girl in year eight,' says Jack.

Dean looks at me, then looks back at them. 'Shut up, you morons.'

They look a bit taken aback. I'm grateful to Dean. It feels weird them going on about Eleanor like that. I mean she is my . . .

What am I thinking about? I've only just gone mad at Andy for using that word. I don't get myself. I don't get anything.

Dean's mum wasn't in so Dean and I pooled what we'd got and it was only enough for one string. I don't really care. My head's spinning with other stuff. All the way back to Sylvia's I keep going over and over what happened at the rehearsal. Then I start thinking back. Further and further back. Trying to remember how come me and Eleanor hate each other so much. It's like I'm peeling off loads of layers of wallpaper to see what colour the wall was in the first place.

I didn't choose Eleanor for the lead.

Why?

Because she doesn't deserve it. She hates me.

Why?

Because I hate her.

Why?

Because she said that stuff about it being my fault that she had to go over to her dad's again.

I'm almost up to their drive, and I can't stop peeling off more layers.

She only said that stuff because she was already mad with me.

Why?

Because I had a go at her sister.

Why?

Because she was just standing there being stupid . . . and her stupid friend had the cheek to talk about Louise's poncy wallpaper – in front of my mates . . .

Just outside the back door I stop because I reckon I've got to the bottom layer now.

No, it wasn't that. It was because of what Andy said. I can still hear his voice . . . *'Oi, Joe! I think your stepsister wants a word with you.'*

But as I push open the door I get this sudden flashback to Kelly Grey in our classroom, with her stupid pouty lips and her drippy voice . . .

'It'll be nice at Eleanor's. And you'll have a brand new mum, won't you?'

The feeling that someone's rammed a knife in my stomach comes back to me. I remember going off to the toilet and hearing Dean going mad at Kelly. *'What'd you have to say that for?'*

And Kelly protesting . . . *'What? I'm only saying what Eleanor said. What's wrong with that?'*

I push open the door. Angry. Eleanor's so dumb – that's the bottom layer. That's why I hate her.

'Hi,' says Sylvia as I go into the kitchen. 'We've got a new arrival!'

Then Jade comes careering in and springs up on me, clinging with her legs like a monkey. 'Telly's here. Mum got him when we were at school as a surprise.' She grips my head with her hands and makes me look at her. 'Why didn't you get off the bus with Ellie and Lou-lou?'

I try to shake her down but it's not easy. She's got good muscles in those thin legs of hers. 'Bought a new string for my guitar.'

She ignores that, jumps off me and grabs my hand. 'Come and see him.'

Louise is in the sitting room with a girl of about Jade's age who's got very blonde hair. They're sitting on the floor, the kitten springing about in the middle of them. It's totally black with bright blue eyes. We had a cat once, called Rolo. It had nine kittens in the airing cupboard, and Mum went out and bought new towels because she didn't want to disturb them all. Mum was like that.

'Don't scare him!' says Jade.

'We're not,' says Louise. 'Isn't he sweet, Joe?'

She's actually spoken to me without sounding scared.

I don't have to answer because they're all glued to Telly. I'm thinking I'd rather be glued to a real telly.

'This is Rosie,' says Jade, plonking herself on the floor next to the kid with the blonde hair.

Louise actually smiles at me.

'Look, he's coming to me!' squeaks Jade. 'He knows I'm his owner already!'

I leave them to it and go upstairs, wondering where Eleanor might be (as if I couldn't guess).

In my room I'm getting out of my school uniform when I hear her through the wall. Crying.

13 THE LIAR

Saturday morning. Ten to seven. I'm wide awake, feeling pants.

I should be feeling great. No school for two days. The house to myself because that lot are all going to their dad's. But I'm not. I feel bad about Eleanor. She stayed in her room for ages yesterday evening, even though Jade kept on trying to persuade her to 'come and play with Telly'.

She doesn't want to go her dad's. I'm trying to convince myself it's not my fault she's going. I mean, it was Sylvia's idea, wasn't it? Then I think about her crying, and half of me wants to go and knock on her door and say, 'Look, can we make a truce?' But the other half is still mad at her. It's that *brand new mum* thing again. I just can't get it out of my head. Leave her to cry. Serves her right.

So yesterday evening, when she eventually came down, anyone could see she'd been crying. I think Jade and Louise had been gagged by Sylvia from saying anything, because they kept on staring at Eleanor, all big-eyed. Jade looked like she was bursting to speak, but stopping herself by pursing her lips really tightly.

It seemed quite funny at the time – not now though. I'm thinking maybe I'll say I'm going to Dean's on Sunday for the whole day. Then if Dad and Sylvia know I'm not even going to be here, they might let Eleanor and the others come back on Saturday night. At least they'd get to see Telly on Sunday that way.

The moment I've had this thought I feel a

whole lot better. I want to tell Dad straight away, so he can tell Sylvia and she can sort it out with Jim. I know what adults are like – they need lots of notice. It's totally quiet when I creep along to their bedroom and knock on the door.

'Come in,' says Sylvia, half asleep.

They probably think it's Jade. They're going to get a shock when they see it's me. I'd better warn them. 'It's Joe!' I whisper with my mouth against the door so no one else wakes up.

There's a bit of scuffling about then Dad says, 'Yeah, come in, Joe.'

It really freaks me out having to look at them both in bed. But this is urgent.

I've learnt my lines. 'I forgot to tell you that Dean's mum invited me to their house for the whole day tomorrow.'

Dad's leaning on his elbow looking at me through one eye, with his mouth open. He's gormless in the mornings, Dad is. 'Right . . .'

Sylvia's got both eyes wide open. 'That'll be good then, Joe. Thanks for letting me know.'

I've got to make sure she's got the message. 'I was thinking about Jade and the others being able to see the kitten and everything.'

Sylvia nods and smiles. 'Yeah. Don't worry about Jade. She flits from one thing to another. I reckon now she's had her fix of Telly she'll be desperate to go and see Jamie and Max.'

'What about . . . the others?'

Sylvia's kind of sussing me out, I can tell. 'Ellie might quite like to be home though.'

Good. That wraps it up. I've done my bit. I turn to go.

'Oh Joe . . .' Dad's still got just the one eye open. 'Stick the kettle on, mate.'

'Ellie doesn't want any breakfast,' Jade tells me, dipping her soldier into her boiled egg very slowly and stirring it round carefully.

Sylvia's making more toast and tea. 'She

might have some when you lot have gone.'

I don't like the sound of this.

'Yeah, when she can get a bit of peace,' says Dad, grinning into his cornflakes bowl. He can say stuff like that these days. Everyone's used to him now.

'Ellie's not going to Dad's. She's staying at home with Telly,' Jade tells me. 'Lucky thing.'

I try not to choke on my toast but I'm thinking maybe I should have thought this through a bit more carefully. I wasn't counting on her being around for the whole weekend. In fact I was thinking that Dean could come over today.

On my way upstairs after breakfast I can see Eleanor in the sitting room. She's lying on her stomach on the rug with a smile on her face, and Telly's crawling on her back. When she sees me the smile vanishes like ice hit by hot water. I think about the truce idea, but only for a nanosecond. She'd probably have a real go at me

– then I'd wish I hadn't bothered, especially as this whole mess is her fault anyway. I guess the only thing that'll make her happy will be if I go out.

A few minutes later when I'm in the bathroom I can hear Jade on the landing giving Eleanor strict instructions to 'guard' her kitten.

'Don't worry,' says Eleanor. Her voice is all soft. She really likes Jade, Eleanor does. 'I'll look after Telly. Come on, let's pack your bag.'

The moment Louise and Jade have gone off with Jim, Sylvia calls out from the hall, 'Nick and I are going shopping. Either of you two want to come with us?'

'I'm staying here to look after Telly,' Ellie answers from the sitting room.

That must be my cue. 'I'm going to Dean's,' I call down from the landing.

Dad comes to the bottom of the stairs. 'Back at lunch time, yeah?'

Sylvia pushes open the sitting-room door. 'You'll be OK on your own for a couple of hours, won't you, love?'

I can't hear what Eleanor says, but it must be 'yes' because next minute Dad and Sylvia are off. Being on my own in the house with Eleanor does my head in so I just belt out the door as fast as I can and don't even take my jacket.

There's no one at home at Dean's place, and I don't feel like going to Andy's or Jack's after what they said about fancying Eleanor, so I go to the shopping centre because I'm freezing cold.

The Gadget Shop has got some cool games and I'm just about to go in when I see Eleanor's reflection in the window. At least I think it's her. It's hard to tell, and no way am I turning round or she'll see me. So I dive into the shop and take a subtle glance through the window, and I'm right. It *is* her. She's on the other side of the centre, walking towards WHSmith. Brilliant. That means I can go home.

I can't wait to have the whole house to myself. I'm going to play music loudly or just flop in front of the telly and help myself to whatever food I want. I break into a jog to get warm.

The moment I'm back I go straight to the bathroom and soak my hands in hot water because my fingers are nearly dropping off I'm so freezing. Then I go into my room and see my guitar and think I might have a play through *Yesterday*. I've got to learn it by heart.

Half an hour later I can sing the whole song and play it at the same time with no music. This is magic. I never thought it would be such a doddle. I'm right in the middle of pretending I'm at Earls Court when I hear the hall door open from the kitchen. I shut up instantly and listen. *Please let it be Dad and Sylvia back from shopping.*

But I never heard a car so I know it can't be

them. I stay completely quiet and still like I'm frozen. Only I can't be *completely* quiet because my heart's making more noise than Woody the Woodpecker.

'Hello?' comes Eleanor's voice, a bit shaky. She'd never be that friendly to me. She must think it's a burglar. I'd better say something back. I'm not looking forward to this.

I go out on to the landing, and at that very moment, I suddenly remember Telly. 'Did you leave Telly on his own?'

She goes a bit pink. 'He was safely in the kitchen. He couldn't come to any harm.'

It's there again – that feeling I got in the music room. I can't help it – I feel sorry for her. I take a breath as deep as the Grand Canyon. 'Do you want to have a run through *Yesterday*?'

For a microsecond there, I could swear she looks like she's about to say 'yes'. But then her eyes harden over. 'What's the point? Kelly's got the lead, thanks to you.'

I think back to what happened in the music room and feel a bit guilty. Then I remember those six stabbing words again – *You'll have a brand new mum.*

I give her my coldest stare. 'I'm going to Dean's.'

There's a silence while she stares at the wall. She doesn't know what to say. Good.

Walking back into town, I'm feeling mad with Eleanor again and wondering why I ever felt sorry for her.

My phone bleeps. It's a text from Andy . . . *Up 2 anything?*

I don't particularly want to see Andy. I'm not in the mood for getting the mickey taken out of me. But I'm bored out of my skull and fed up with wandering round on my own. I know Andy though. When he sends you texts like this it usually means he wants to come to *your* house because he's hacked off with his own.

And no way is he coming to Sylvia's house while Eleanor's there.

I text him back . . . *Just going into town. Meet you outside Gadget Shop.*

But a minute later my phone rings and it's him. 'I don't want to go into town, Joe. I haven't got any money.' *Uh-oh.* 'I'll come round to your place, OK?'

No way! Not with Eleanor there! 'Trouble is, Dad's doing some work – you know, all over the house – because we've got a leak. The place is practically under water.' I'm feeling quite pleased with that.

'Hang on a sec . . .'

I can hear muffled talking.

'Who are you talking to?'

'Jack. He says let's go up to the rec.'

Result!

'OK, see you there.'

So I turn round again because the rec's quite near Sylvia's. And as I'm walking along, my mind goes straight back to Eleanor and Kelly Grey. I'm picturing Eleanor's face when I was on the bus and she'd just got off with Louise. She was looking all sad, staring straight ahead in a kind of trance. She was probably gutted about Kelly getting the lead in the band. I stop walking and stare at the ground. I'm thinking about Kelly now. Something's whizzing round in my brain. I'm trying to get it to stay still so I can focus on it . . .

That look on Kelly's face when I refused to join the band because of Eleanor being in it — like she was pleased. But she still got me to join, didn't she? And how did she do it? By telling me that Eleanor said I wouldn't be any good. I'm getting cross now because I've got the feeling I've been used. Kelly only wanted me in the band because she knew Eleanor and me had started to hate each other's guts. That meant she could be pretty certain that when it came to choosing who was going to be lead, I'd choose her.

It's driving me mad all this stuff in my head. How am I ever going to find out the truth?

Then out of the blue I think about Eleanor and Louise getting off the bus. Those words of Andy's . . . *'Say 'bye-bye to your stepsisters, then.'*

My reply . . . *'They're not my stepsisters.'*

Was Eleanor hacked off because of *that*? I dunno. All I know is that I used to like her and she used to like me. So how come it's all gone wrong?

14 INSTINCT

'Hey, Joe! *You* look happy!' Jack falls about laughing at his incredible wit.

Andy grins and bashes me on the back. 'Come on, mate, spit it out! What's bugging you? You've got droopier chops than a St Bernard's.'

I hadn't realised it was that obvious.

'Nothing. Just bored.'

'Well, look who it is!' Jack suddenly says, stopping in his tracks.

Andy and I follow his gaze.

Oh God!

'Eleanor Stern! What's she doing?' says

Andy, squinting because the sun's come out and it's bright.

'Looks like she's doing a bit of serious training,' says Jack, smirking.

I'm not laughing. I'm worried. She's running and she seems scared and I'm wondering if someone's chasing her. But then I realise it's the other way round. *She's* chasing *someone*. Or rather, some*thing*.

Jack's noticed Telly too. 'Look – she's running after that little cat.'

'She'll never catch it,' says Andy. 'It's got a bit of a head start!'

I've got to help her. But I can't. She'll tell me to get lost and make me feel a right idiot in front of Jack and Andy. No, she'll just have to manage on her own. Serves her right for being so bolshie before.

But if anything happened to Telly, it'd do Eleanor's head in. *And* Louise's. *And* Jade's.

Make sure you guard my kitten, Ellie, won't you?

Don't worry, I'll look after Telly.

'It's gone up that tree!' Jack sniggers. 'Great! We can watch her climb up after it!'

Then Andy spots the burger van. 'Anyone got any cash? I'm starving.'

Jack rattles his pocket with a jammy look on his face. 'I've got half my allowance in here.'

'Fancy seeing you lot!' We all turn round at the sound of Dean's voice. He comes jogging up. 'Thanks for inviting me to the party!'

'I went round your house earlier,' I told him, 'but you weren't there.'

'Yes I was, only I don't wake up unless you hammer the door down.'

So then we're all strolling over to the burger van, me and Dean behind the other two.

'Hey Dean, what would you do if you wanted to know if something was true or not, but you've got no way of finding out?'

He gives me a sideways squint. 'Er . . . I think I'd just go on my instincts.'

'Right . . .'

Something clicks into place. I think it might be my instincts. I stand there rooted to the spot. Dean doesn't notice because the smell of burgers is like a magnet to him. I wait till the three of them are going through all the prices with the burger guy, then I turn round to look for Eleanor. At first I can't see her anywhere and reckon she must have got Telly and gone, but then I get a shock because I spot her halfway up the tree.

'What are you having, Joe?' Dean asks me.

'What? Oh, nothing.' *I couldn't swallow anything right now because of the lump in my throat.* 'Not hungry.'

'What are you looking at?' Then he sees her too. 'What's she doing?'

'Trying to rescue our cat.'

My eyes are really popping now because she's so high and it doesn't look safe to me. If I was on my own I'd get over there and help her, but I can't – not with these three watching. Next minute my stomach flips over because she's slipped and she's hanging from a branch looking terrified. Then she dropped to the ground. Even from over here I can hear her yell out. She's sitting down clutching her ankle. Right, that's it. I don't care what anyone thinks any more.

I sprint over there like I'm trying to win a race.

'Oi! Joe!'

I don't even bother to turn round, just drop down beside her. 'Are you OK?'

Her eyes look terrible – all those emotions packed in again. Only this time they're turned full on me.

'Is it your ankle? D'you think you've twisted it?'

She nods. 'I can't put any weight on it.'

'Here.' I take hold of her ankle and use the same technique that Dad's used twice on me. 'This is what Dad does. It worked for me.' She's trying to be brave but I can tell it's hurting her. I keep pressing and rubbing and twisting it really gently.

Then she looks right at me. And it reminds me of Louise getting the courage together to ask if I wanted a cup of tea. 'I've lost Telly. He's up in the tree.'

'I know. I saw you chasing him.'

'Can you try and get him down?'

'Yeah. I'm just doing this first. There. Try that.' I help her up and she clutches on to me.

From the burger van comes a big 'Woooooo!' from Andy.

'Ignore him. He's a moron.'

'I thought he was your friend.'

'He is, but he's a moron.'

She looks puzzled. Girls must be different. I try to explain. 'It's only like Kelly Grey. You think she's a pain, but she's still your friend.'

She looks me right in the eyes. 'Kelly Grey's no friend of mine.'

'I thought it was just a thing . . . to do with the band . . .'

'It *is*, but it's more than that. To do with you and me. She can't stand it that we live together. She's jealous of me. It makes me so wild.'

I think about Andy and Jack. 'I know the feeling.'

She's really looking at me intently. 'Do you?'

'Yeah. Jack and Andy are always on about you. It's embarrassing. You know . . .'

She nearly smiles at me. Nearly. 'I know, because I'm practically your . . .' then her face clouds right over and her eyes go hard. 'Oh no – I'm not allowed to say that, am I?'

'What?'

She shakes my arm off. 'Nothing.'

There's a silence then I remember Telly. I stick two fingers in my mouth and do one of my loud whistles.

'What are you doing?'

'I need some help for the rescue operation.'

Dean and the other two come jogging over.

'What's going on?' asks Jack, who's first to get to us.

'We've lost our cat,' I tell him. 'He's called Telly.'

Jack and Andy are both gawping at Eleanor. I wish they wouldn't.

'I'm going to climb up and try and get it. When I've got it, I might need some help bringing it down.'

Andy's looking gormless.

'Like one of you getting on the other one's back and reaching up to take it from me.'

'OK,' says Dean.

So up I go. My hands hurt like mad because this is rough bark and it's not that easy to get a grip. I'm showing off a bit trying to go fast, so my legs are copping a load of grazing.

I can see Telly on a high branch. I bet if cats could giggle, that's what he'd be doing now. He's staring at me intently and I'm wondering what he's thinking. 'Here, boy!' I say in a nice encouraging tone. 'Come on.' I reach my hand out and he arches his back and tries to get away. 'It's OK, Telly. Come on.'

But he just arches his back even more. Very slowly I shuffle a bit higher. The stupid cat isn't going to come walking along to me and sit obligingly on my shoulder while I climb down, so I'm just going to have to try and grab it.

I ease myself forward about a centimetre and Telly calmly leaps up to the next branch and walks along to the very end, then starts mucking about like a high-wire artist.

Big gasps from below, and I clearly hear Andy say, 'That's it. He'll never get it now.'

'It's going to kill itself doing stunts like that,' Jack informs us in a great loud voice.

Poor Eleanor must be feeling terrible. 'No he won't!' I call down.

That shuts them all up. But I'm wishing I hadn't sounded so snappy, because I'm going to look a right idiot unless I save this cat, and I haven't the faintest clue how to go about it now.

Then I suddenly remember something Mum said when I was only little and we were in her friend's house. Mum and the friend were chatting away and I would have been bored out of my skull if it hadn't been for these four cats that Mum's friend had got. I was trying desperately to get near enough to at least one of them to pick it up, but they all ran a mile when they saw me crouching down, calling to them.

'Don't open your eyes so wide, Joe,' Mum said. 'Cats narrow their eyes like this, as a sign of friendship.' Then she'd shown me. 'And don't chase after them. Let them come to you. Just sit very still and pretend you're not interested.' So I'd sat on the settee and stared at the wall opposite and counted every single spot on Mum's friend's wallpaper. And sure enough, one of the cats jumped straight up on to my lap and settled there, curled and purring, and another one rubbed itself against my legs.

I wonder if that'll work now. It's my only hope so I'll have to give it a go. I try to look like I'm relaxing – *Oh yeah, in a tree!* – and every so often I give Telly one of those narrow-eyed looks, then I look away again.

'What's he doing up there?' Andy's voice comes ringing out. 'Meditation?'

Someone shushes him. I think it's Eleanor.

'Oh yeah, I forgot he's all trained up in cat psychology, isn't he?' says Jack. He thinks he's so witty.

I ignore that and concentrate on keeping still. Can cats tell when you're uptight? I don't know. I try and make my mind go blank just in case.

And into the blankness come Eleanor's words . . .

'I'm practically your . . . Oh no, I'm not allowed to say that, am I?'

I know now what she was going to say. I

didn't need my instinct to sort out this last piece of the puzzle. And that's why she's upset, isn't it? She's hurting because she knows I don't want to be in her family. I don't want anyone to say that she's my stepsister.

'Look!' Dean whispers from below. I'd been staring down, but I look up and I can't believe my eyes. Telly's only walking towards me. I don't move a muscle. Not even a tendon. I hold my breath as he steps on to my shoulder.

So now I've got two choices. Keep calm and start to climb down, risking Telly leaping off me the moment I move, or make a grab for him so he can't get away, and risk not being able to get down myself.

I wish Mum was here. She'd know what I ought to do. Maybe I'll just sit here a while longer till he completely trusts me.

'Come on then, Joe!' calls Andy. 'Bring it down.'

'He can't, dur,' says Dean. 'It'll jump off.'

'Well, hold on to it with one hand then,' says Andy the know-all.

'Yeah, like he can climb down one-handed,' says Jack.

'Ssh! He knows what he's doing.' That's Eleanor.

And she's right. I *do* know what I'm doing. I didn't mean it to happen like this, but Telly has just given me the answer. He's such a wickedly intelligent cat, he's gone creeping down inside the front of my jacket. It's zipped up so he's nicely wedged. Right, I'll give it another minute.

I count to sixty, not wanting it to come to an end because that means I've got to move into the high risk bit. I can hear Telly purring away right next to my chest. He's not stupid, this kitten. Found himself a nice cosy place out of the cold. And me, I'm freezing. My fingers feel numb. I move about a centimetre at a time, and in a way, I'm quite glad I've got Telly as an excuse, because this tree isn't exactly the easiest in the world to climb down.

'You're doing really well,' Eleanor says softly when I guess I've covered about half the distance.

'Shall I get on Jack's back?' Dean asks me.

'No, it's OK.'

The others don't say anything. My legs start to shake when I get near the bottom. It's because I'm scared Telly's going to scramble out at the last minute. I glance down and see I've run out of branches. I'm standing on the bottom one, about two metres off the ground. I'll crush him if I go down this last bit clinging to the trunk. There's only one thing for it. I take a deep breath, and go for a backwards jump, clutching his wriggling body tightly through my jacket.

'Watch out!' screams Andy, leaping out of the way.

He's too late. I knock him over then land in a heap on the ground and feel a bit of a jarring in my shoulder and both my ankles. I don't know if it's relief because I've finally made it, but I sit there on the muddy grass, clutching the violently wriggling Telly, and crack up laughing. 'That's got you back for all those comments you aimed at me up there.'

Andy gets up, grumbling. Dean and Eleanor crouch down on either side of me. Eleanor reaches inside my jacket. It's a big relief when she's got Telly safely in her hands. 'Come on, you naughty kitten. Let's go home.'

She goes striding off and I'm left staring after her.

'Nice one, Joe,' says Dean, hauling me to my feet.

'You jammy sod, Joe!' says Jack quietly. 'I wish she'd put her hands inside *my* jacket.'

There's something about the way Eleanor's back stiffens that makes me think she heard that.

I roll my eyes at him. 'Shut up, Jack. That's my stepsister you're talking about.'

She turns round and stares at me like she can't

believe her ears. Then very slowly she breaks into a great big smile. My instinct was right.

I catch up with her and fall into step. Dean's on the other side. The other two are behind.

We're nearly home when Andy gets a text from his mum telling him to come straight back for lunch. Dean and Jack say they'd better get going too.

So that just leaves me and Eleanor.

15 TAKING THE LEAD

I get the mugs out while Eleanor puts the
kettle on.

'Joe?'

I wait.

'Sorry about what I said about you going
away for the weekend instead of us. I didn't
mean to upset you about your mum . . .'

'It's OK.' I want to try and talk about
everything I've been feeling for the last few
weeks, but it seems too big to explain, so I just
say, 'Forget it.'

Then she says, 'Can I just ask you one

thing about your mum?'

I nod.

She bites her lip and looks at the carpet. 'Was it the second of May when she died?'

I frown, not getting her. 'No, fourteenth of January. Why?'

'So what's the second of May then?'

I suddenly click and go bright red. 'Nah, that's nothing. I did it . . . by mistake.'

'Shall I Tippex it out then?'

'Yeah, if you want.'

'No, if *you* want.' She's looking at me intently.

I nod.

She pours the boiling water into the teapot. 'It must be . . . awful for you . . .'

'What?'

She answers so quietly I hardly hear. 'Not having a mum.'

I'm remembering what Kelly said all that time ago in the classroom.

'Kelly once said that you said . . . I'd be

getting a brand new mum living here . . .'

Eleanor slams the kettle down and looks like thunder for a second, then she sits down at the table and rests her head on her hands, like she can't take any more. 'That stupid girl! You *do* believe that I'd never ever say such a horrible thing, don't you?'

The relief is incredible. 'Yeah. Course I do.'

She looks up. There are tears in her eyes. 'No wonder you hated me so much.'

'That's history. It's just Kelly who's cocked things up . . . and my mates taking the mickey. At least we've got it sorted now.'

She still looks miserable.

Maybe this'll cheer her up. 'Pass us the Tippex.'

She smiles, but only just.

On Sunday evening Jade comes crashing in and I think what a lot's happened in one week.

'Thanks for guarding him, Ellie.'

'Pleasure.' Eleanor and I exchange a grin.

Louise catches it and her pale face goes all pink.

'Did you have a nice time?' I ask her.

She nods happily.

'Have you been playing your guitar in the mirror, Joe?' asks Jade, stroking Telly.

'That's enough, Jade,' says Sylvia. Then she quickly tries to change the subject in case I'm feeling embarrassed (which I am, but not half as much as I would have been a week ago). 'What's the song you're doing for the concert, Joe?'

'*Yesterday*.'

'Play it for us now, Joe?' says Louise. 'And Ellie can sing.'

'I don't really . . .' Eleanor begins to say.

'Go on,' I try and persuade her.

She doesn't say no, so I go and get my guitar.

Dad makes everyone sit down like a proper audience.

When Eleanor starts singing it shocks me. Her voice is about a million times better than it was last time – a billion times better than Kelly Grey's.

I keep my eye on my guitar because I have to watch what I'm doing to cover the right frets, but after a little while I can't help looking up.

Sylvia's got tears in her eyes. The others are all staring. Louise is hugging her knees. She's pinker than ever.

The song is completely changed from when we did it in the music room. I'm playing it loads better than I would have done if I'd spent the whole weekend practising on my own. There's just nothing boring about it any more. Now I know what was wrong with it on Friday – something beginning with K.

When we finish the whole family breaks into applause.

'You should be proud of yourselves,' says Sylvia. 'Really proud.'

Eleanor's looking at me, like she's waiting for me to speak.

I grin at her. 'I don't suppose you've got Chris Counter's number? I've got something to tell him.'

'Who's Chris Counter?' asks Jade.

'What have you got to tell him?' That's Louise.

'That I'm not playing in the band till he changes the lead singer.'

I look at Eleanor. I'm expecting her to be really pleased. I reckon she is, but there's something else. Maybe I won't phone Chris till I've had the chance to talk to her.

Later, when I'm up in my room, there's a knock on my door. I call out 'Come in.' It's Eleanor. She closes the door and leans against it, looking anxious.

'You know the band . . .'

I wait.

'Well, can you do me a favour?'

'Yeah, what?'

'Don't phone Chris . . .'

So I was right.

'Why not? You're miles better than Kelly.'

'I've been thinking about it, though. The thing is, she's always been jealous of me – not just because of you, because of me.'

'What do you mean?'

'Well, she's not very popular . . . and she's not very good at anything . . . and . . .'

She's biting her lip. I wait.

'. . . and I think it would be really horrible of me to take the lead away from her.'

I can't believe this. I've been through hell because of Kelly Grey, so has Eleanor. And now she wants to let her off the hook.

'But Kelly's really stirred things up, you know . . .'

'Yeah, I know.'

'I'm not so sure you do, actually. I mean, d'you realise how she got me to join the band?'

Eleanor narrows her eyes. 'How?'

'She said *you* said I wouldn't be any good!'

Eleanor looks embarrassed. Then she smiles. 'It worked though, didn't it? I knew you'd like the challenge.'

I feel my hackles rising and I'm about to go off on one, when I realise something.

'Did you *want* me to join the band, then?'

'Course I did. I knew you were good. Your dad told me.'

I look at her and can't help grinning, but then I'm back to what we were talking about. 'But are you sure you want Kelly to be lead singer?'

She nods slowly. All her emotions are piled into her eyes again.

Only this time when she switches them on me, I get the best feeling.

What happens next in the step-chain?
Meet Eleanor in . . .

Step-Chain

CHANGING
MY
NAME

1 ANGER BUBBLES

Cliff Richard was blaring out from the speakers and the room was filled with happy noises. People were chatting, eating and drinking. Mum in her lovely cream wedding dress and Nick in his silvery grey suit were amongst the couples dancing in romantic slow clinches.

I could tell by Mum and Nick's lips that they were singing along with Cilff's words while they gazed into each other's eyes. Yuk!

As I watched them I felt the old familiar bubbles of anger starting to pop just under my ribs. Not because they'd just got married – I was totally cool with that. I love them both like mad.

No, it's just my stupid hang-up.

It all started about two weeks ago in our kitchen at home. Well, actually it didn't. It started long before that, but it came to a head two weeks ago.

Mum and I were sitting at the table. She was testing me on my French future tense, only she seemed to be doodling at the same time. I couldn't see properly because her arm was in the way. Then she got up to put the kettle on and I saw that she'd written *Sylvia Stern*, which is her name, and then beside it *Sylvia Evans*, which is what she'd be called if she decided to change to Nick's name when they married.

It's funny, but I'd never thought about that before, and it was only then that I clicked.

'Oh, yeah . . .' I said, my brain slowly moving away from French verbs and getting into marriages. 'You won't be Sylvia Stern any more, will you?'

Mum laughed. 'Don't look so shocked, love!'

'I'm not.'

And I wasn't. I mean, we all know lots of people change their name when they get married. It was just that for some unknown reason I'd never thought it through in connection with Mum until now. It was going to be so weird. In two weeks' time I'd have a different surname from my own mum.

She came back to the table with cups of tea for both of us and asked me what the French for *I will give* was, but I couldn't concentrate any more because the words *Nick and Sylvia Evans* were dancing about inside my brain, blotting out everything else.

In the end, when I kept on coming out with wrong answers, Mum said I ought to give it a break and try again later, so I went up to my room and sat on the floor leaning against my bed. Through the bedroom wall I could her my stepbrother, Joe, practising his guitar. It sounded really good.

I started reciting all the names in this family in my head – Nick Evans, Sylvia Evans, Joe Evans, Eleanor Stern, Louise Stern, Jade Stern. But I don't want to be a Stern, and I don't want Louise and Jade to be Sterns either. I want all of us to have the same surname – Evans. This is where we live, after all. This family is our main family. Louise and Jade and I only go over to Dad's once a fortnight at the weekend, and *I* only go over on the Sunday these days, because it's got so boring lately and Dad treats me like a baby.

As I sat there listening to Joe's guitar, something suddenly hit me. I didn't know why I hadn't thought of it straight away. I leapt to my feet and belted downstairs to the kitchen.

Mum was loading the dishwasher.

'Can I change my name too, to Evans, like you, Mum?' I blurted out. Then I stood there all tense and excited, shoulders hunched like a little kid, waiting for her to turn round, break into a big smile and say, *Of course you can, darling. I'm so pleased you want to be like me.*

But she didn't even turn round, just started wiping the draining board. 'I don't think your dad'd be very impressed with that idea, love!'

I watched as thin swirls of soapy water swished out from the J-cloth, and felt the anger bubbles burst inside me for the first time.

'You don't seem to realise – this is a big important thing to me, Mum. Can you just ask Dad?'

She did turn round then, but it was obvious she'd already decided my idea was no good. 'Well, I can always ask him, I suppose, but – '

'Can you phone him straight away?'

'You *are* keen, aren't you?' she said, shaking her head, with a little smile on her face. 'I shouldn't raise your hopes, Ellie. I can tell you now the answer will be no.'

'But why do we always have to do what Dad says? He's not in charge, *you* are.'

'You can't just go ahead and do something like that without even consulting Dad. He'd be really upset.'

'What about *me*? *I'll* be really upset if I don't change it.'

'Well, I'll mention it to him next time I phone him, but not tonight. It's too late.'

I had to be satisfied with that for the moment. But there was something else I wanted to sort out too.

'Have you phoned Tasha's mum about me staying there while you and Nick are on your honeymoon?'

Mum started putting things away in the corner cupboard. 'I . . . er . . . decided it would be a bit much asking Tasha's mum to have you for three days.'

'Oh *Mum*!' I started to wail.

'She works full time, Ellie . . . and it isn't fair

on her, especially when you've got a perfectly good father who always loves to see you – '

'Oh, *no*! Don't tell me you've arranged for me to stay at Dad's. I don't believe it!'

'Well, Jade and Louise are going to be there. And as Dad said, it's sensible to have the three of you under the same roof.'

I was furious. Dad *again*. 'I bet it was him who said I wasn't allowed to stay at Tasha's, wasn't it, and you're just making it up about Tasha's mum working full time and everything?'

'We sorted it out together, Dad and I.'

But I didn't believe her. There's a girl at school called Mel, whose parents are divorced, and she once told me that if her dad didn't get his own way as far as she and her brother and sister were concerned, he just gave her mum less money. I've got the feeling Dad might be doing that too. Mel said it happens in all split families. I once asked Mum about it but she went tight-lipped and said it was none of my business, which makes me even more sure I'm right.

'He really does my head in, Mum, laying the law down all the time. It's so unfair. I'm not a baby. I'm thirteen years old and I don't even get a say in where I'm staying while you're away.'

'Calm down, Ellie. It's decided and that's that. Anyway, I bet you'll have a great time. Dad's planned some really fun things.'

'Oh halleluiah! They might be fun things if you're six like Jade, or seven like the twins, but I'm telling you, they are *not* fun for me.'

Mum got a bit stressy then. 'Well, Louise always loves being at Dad's – and she's only eighteen months younger than you.'

I went mad. 'That's because she's that kind of person – all shy and quiet. Oh come on, Mum! I told you how embarrassing it is the way Dad treats me, giving me a set bedtime on a Saturday night and not letting me stay in the house on my own. I can't even have Tash over because . . .' I went off into a *blah blah*

blah voice, '. . . I can see her any time.'

Mum sighed and looked suddenly tired. She pursed her lips and I knew there was no point in saying anything else for now. I also knew I'd hit the nail on the head. It was Dad who was behind all this.

I scowled and shut the door a bit harder than usual.

And here we were two weeks later at Mum and Nick's wedding. Dad has got his own way in everything. Even though I've pestered and pestered Mum, I'm definitely not allowed to change my name because *Dad* says I can't, *and* I've got to suffer three whole days being treated like a baby and doing 'fun' (ha ha!) things because Dad thinks it's better that we're all three under the same roof. And now Sylvia Evans, with her brand new name, is dancing with her brand new husband while her daughter, Eleanor Stern, sits and watches . . .

Collect the links in the step-chain . . .

 1. To see her dad, Sarah has to stay with the woman who wrecked her family. Will she do it? Find out in *One Mum Too Many!*

 2. Ollie thinks a holiday with girls will be a nightmare. And it is, because he's fallen for his stepsister. Can it get any worse? Find out in *You Can't Fancy Your Stepsister*

 3. Lissie's half-sister is a spoilt brat, but her mum thinks she's adorable. Can Lissie make her see what's really going on? Find out in *She's No Angel*

4. Becca's mum describes her boyfriend's daughter as perfect in every way. Can Becca bear to meet her? Find out in *Too Good To Be True*

 5. Ed's stepsisters are getting seriously on his nerves. Should he go and live with his mum? Find out in *Get Me Out Of Here*

 6. Hannah and Rachel are stepsisters. They're also best friends. What will happen to them if their parents split up? Find out in *Parents Behaving Badly*

 7. When Bethany discovers the truth about Robby, she knows her family will go ballistic. Is it possible to keep his secret from them? Find out in *Don't Tell Mum*

8. Ryan's life is made hell by his bullying stepbrother. Has he got the guts to stand up for himself? Find out in *Losing My Identity*

9. Katie knows it's wrong to lie to her mum. Will she decide to own up, despite the consequences? Find out in *Secrets and Lies*

10. Ashley can't stand her mum's interfering boyfriend. But it's possible she's got him wrong. Has she? Find out in *Healing the Pain*

12. Eleanor wants to change her name. But her dad won't let her. Will she get her own way? Find out in *Changing My Name*